Alec Maso

And whatever the story was, it was due to Claire. And the invitation Claire had received to spend the weekend with Miranda Craig. The hometown star who refused to talk to the local paper.

"Have you read Miranda Craig's autobiography?" Lissa asked. "Our Claire is in it."

"Claire?" When Alec turned to her, she had taken her glasses off and was shaking her chestnut hair loose from its ponytail. For a split second Claire seemed like someone who could hold her own with the hottest female star on the planet. Then she put her glasses back on, pushed her hair back behind her ears and slumped her shoulders again.

"Missy Craig was my best friend," Claire said.

"Do you know how much getting that interview would mean for this paper?" Alec insisted.

Lissa interrupted. "What Claire is trying to tell you, Alec, is that *she* isn't speaking to Miranda. Miranda stole Claire's fiancé."

"You had a fiancé?" Alec sputtered.

"Claire had a few fiancés," Lissa added. "Miranda stole them all."

Alec absorbed the shock of the words. "We're going after this story."

"Miranda is not going to spill her secrets to some reporter I drag along," Claire insisted.

Alec smiled triumphantly. "But I won't be there as a reporter. I'll be your fiancé."

Dear Reader,

A new year always brings lots of new friends and new opportunities into our lives. At LOVE & LAUGHTER we are especially proud of the number of new writers we have discovered. One of the greatest joys an editor can have is making "the call"—telling a hopeful, unpublished author, "We love your book and want to buy it."

Tracy South is one of those new voices. She is also the winner of the LOVE & LAUGHTER contest. Her book is a real delight, both witty and romantic. Other new voices in the months ahead include Stephanie Bond, Bonnie Tucker, Trish Jensen and Colleen Collins. I'm sure you'll enjoy their stories as much as we did and look for books by these fresh, new funny ladies.

Prolific and always popular Jacqueline Diamond delivers a knockout punch in the hilarious *Punchline*. This story about rival editors from competing magazines, who just *despise* each other yet keep ending up together, is terrific. A classic battle of the sexes, set in the 1990s.

I hope the New Year brings you much love and laughter.

Malle Vallik

Malle Vallik
Associate Senior Editor

THE FIANCÉ THIEF
Tracy South

Harlequin Books

TORONTO • NEW YORK • LONDON
AMSTERDAM • PARIS • SYDNEY • HAMBURG
STOCKHOLM • ATHENS • TOKYO • MILAN
MADRID • WARSAW • BUDAPEST • AUCKLAND

ISBN 0-373-44012-X

THE FIANCÉ THIEF

Copyright © 1997 by Tracy Jones

When Harlequin announced its Love & Laughter contest for unpublished authors, it seemed like an omen that Carole Lombard's name was mentioned in the write-up. Not only am I a total fanatic about her films, I actually owe the idea of *The Fiancé Thief* to one of her roles. While watching *Twentieth Century*, I was struck by how much a college friend resembled her. I hadn't talked to this friend since she moved to New York to become an actress. What if she became famous one day? Well, I'd be happy for her. No plot there. But what if she were someone I didn't like? How would I feel then?

Comic novelist P. G. Wodehouse said someone told him, "Get the love story straight and the comedy will fall into place." I hope you'll find I've gotten it right on both counts. Enjoy!

—Tracy South

To my daughter, Dylan

1

ALEC MASON COULD SMELL a story. He wouldn't have claimed to have anything as sissy as intuition or as goofy as ESP. He wouldn't even admit to having a nose for news, because he was a precise man, one who despised clichés. But there was no denying that right here, right now, he was being teased by the scent of some breaking event. And whatever the story was, it was unfolding here in his office.

He leaned against the door and surveyed his trio of reporters. Granted, they didn't look any more inspired than usual. Hank was bent over his keyboard, his usual calm expression on his face. Lissa was making faces at her computer, and Alec watched her as she typed a word, then rested her head on the desk. Every sentence was sheer torture for Lissa. Although Alec didn't share her agony, he did admire her gift for melodrama.

He shifted his gaze to Claire, seated at her cluttered desk about five feet away from Hank and Lissa. No melodrama here. Claire Morgan was always achingly earnest and deathly serious. He watched her as her hands flew across the keyboard, her face screwed up in an unholy frown at the screen. Her hair was pulled back into a messy ponytail, and her glasses slipped down a little on her face as she typed.

How such a drab girl could turn in such sparkling copy was a mystery to him. He had hired her, sight unseen, on the basis of clips she'd sent to him. It was one of the few times his instincts had led him astray. He had been so knocked out by her writing, and he'd been so afraid that the town's other, bigger paper would snap her up that he had called her with a job offer the second he'd finished reading her clips. From her confident purr on the phone, and the brassy edge to her words on the page, he'd pictured a vivacious, hard-hitting, seasoned journalist. Instead, he was stuck with a stammering mouse.

So far he had her limited to life-style stories, although that wasn't what he'd planned when he hired her. Even Claire could get quotes from the chatty women at the Ladies' Gardening Club. And good quotes they were, he had to admit. But there was no way he was going to send her out after real news. He could just picture it: "Excuse me, Mr. Mayor, sir, I hate to bother you, and I don't mean to hurt your feelings, but..." The other paper, the city's daily, would have the story and its follow-up headed for the recycling bin before she ever got through her apologies.

Hank and Lissa were still oblivious to his presence, but Claire seemed to sense his stare. When she turned and saw him by the door, she started a little and let out a nearly inaudible yelp. Blushing, she turned back to the computer, but the commotion made the two other reporters look up.

"Did I forget to shave today, Claire?" His voice boomed and echoed in the quiet room. "My looks don't usually terrify women and children."

She didn't look at him. "Sorry," she said in a small voice. "I didn't see you standing there."

"Spying, Alec?" Lissa asked.

"I was trying to see how many words you could write before you fainted dead away," he told her. "I see you haven't reached your limit."

"The day's young," Lissa told him. "And I'm only seventy-five words into my story."

Hank looked up from his computer. "We'll have an ambulance here yet."

Claire was ignoring the others' banter, typing furiously again. "What are you working on, Claire?"

Damned if she didn't turn bright red again. He'd dealt with some coy women in his day, but never had he met one who turned into a nervous heap every time he glanced at her. It was beginning to get on his nerves.

Not giving her a chance to answer, he went on. "You know, when I walked in here just a few minutes ago, I had the feeling that something had happened here today. Could that have something to do with what you're working on, Claire?"

"No, it doesn't." She sounded honest enough when she said it, but her glance darted almost imperceptibly to one corner of her desk. Alec saw that Hank and Lissa also looked toward that same corner. In a flash, he was there, and he immediately zeroed in on the newest addition to Claire's massive pile of junk. There, sticking out from under a stack of film guides, surrounded by disposable containers from yesterday's lunch, sat a registered letter. He had just one twinge of conscience before his newsman's hunger got to him.

He picked it up. "Tell me this is nothing I should be interested in, and I'll believe you," he told Claire, who jumped up from her seat and grabbed at the letter.

"You can't read that," she said, plainly evading the issue of whether or not he'd be interested in the letter's contents. Just as he'd suspected, Claire was a lousy liar. Another reason why she'd never make a good reporter.

He held the letter aloft. "Tell me I wouldn't be interested," he repeated.

Claire's eyes were bright and angry behind her glasses, and her hair was slipping out of its impromptu ponytail. She put her hands on her hips, and when she did so, Alec was surprised to notice the swell of her chest and the outline of her tiny waist, attributes that had been hidden by her baggy cotton dress. A rosy color had sneaked into her

cheeks, and he took a second to notice the way it highlighted her creamy pale skin.

What was he thinking? This was the oldest diversion in
the book. It would take more accomplished feminine wiles
than Claire Morgan's to make that trick work.

"It's a federal offense to read someone else's mail," she
said.

Alec looked at Hank, who packed in his brain every ar-
cane fact worth knowing, as well as a wealth of those that
weren't. Hank shook his head.

"It's only an offense to interfere with its delivery," he
said. As Alec started to slip the letter out of its envelope,
Hank continued. "However, what Lissa did, pretending to
be Claire and signing for the letter, might actually fall into
that category."

Alec stopped, the letter halfway out, and turned to
Lissa. She shrugged, and her contact-blue eyes widened.
"I don't know how on earth I heard the man say 'Lissa
Barnard.' I was halfway through the letter before I realized it surely wasn't meant for me. And then, since I was
just getting to the interesting part..." Her voice trailed off,
and she smiled apologetically.

Alec slid the letter all the way back into the envelope,
and handed it back to Claire. He put a comforting hand on
her shoulder and took a slightly malicious delight in her
resulting tremble. "For you, Claire, to think for a moment that I would ever read mail addressed to you. For you
to even consider that I would use and abuse my employees
in that way. It's an arrow to the heart, that's what it is."

He took his hand off her shoulder and looked at Lissa.
"Well?" he asked.

Claire said, "Lissa, you can't," just as Lissa said, less
sincerely, "Oh, Alec, I can't." He raised his eyebrows at
Lissa. It took her all of three seconds to crack.

"Really, Claire, what can I do? He's my boss, after all."
Alec saw Claire roll her eyes. "And even though you've

just been working here a few months, you know what this would mean to him."

Now his curiosity was really piqued. Lissa, as he knew she would, told the story in her dramatic, drawn-out way. There was no use rushing her, so he simply listened.

"Have you read Miranda Craig's autobiography?" Lissa asked.

It was with a sinking feeling that he answered no. The name Miranda Craig meant nothing but trouble to him. The biggest female box-office draw in the country just happened to be from their town. That ought to give the papers there a right to an exclusive or two, right? Some kind of hometown indulgence? But because of a bad review she'd gotten from the daily paper as the lead in a college play, she'd refused to deal with any local media, and had also forbidden her family to talk to them. Even the relatives who regularly spilled to the tabloids refused to talk to Alec, or his boss, publisher Mick Regan. It wasn't fair, considering that their paper, a weekly, hadn't even been around when Miranda Craig was giving her legendary hammy performance in *Uncle Vanya*.

"In the unlikely event that Miranda Craig agrees to an interview, I'll read her book. I don't have to put myself through that torture otherwise."

"Well," Lissa said, clearly warming to her subject. "Our Claire gets a good bit of space in Miranda Craig's book."

"Claire?" When Alec turned to her, she had taken her glasses off and was shaking her chestnut hair loose from its ponytail. For a split second, Claire struck him as someone who could hold her own with the hottest female star on the planet. Then she put her glasses back on, pushed her hair back behind her ears and slumped her shoulders again.

"Missy Craig, as I knew her, was my best friend."

He sputtered a little as he spoke. "Miranda, or whatever the hell her name was, was your best friend, and you never told me?"

She shrugged. Not, he decided, very apologetically.

"Do you know how much getting that interview would mean for this paper's clout?" He started to pace, his body tense and his blood rushing in his ears. He might have thought he was coming down with a bad case of the weekend flu if these sensations didn't have a tinge of familiarity. He'd felt like this often when he'd been a reporter for a large daily in Atlanta. His beat was small but he covered it well, and he learned there to feel the rightness of a story. When Mick, his college journalism professor and mentor, had offered him the editorship of the weekly he'd bought, he'd come back to Ridgeville expecting there would be lots of days when he felt like this. Could he have ever guessed then that he, the man who was going to be Woodward and Bernstein rolled together, would be salivating at the thought of interviewing an actress? His loss of cool was not only out of character, it was decidedly unprofessional. He snapped his mouth shut.

He couldn't quite decipher the look Claire gave him. "Are you finished?" she asked. When he nodded, she said, "I didn't tell you about my friendship with Missy because it isn't relevant."

"Isn't relevant?" So much for playing it cool. "You played Barbie dolls with the most powerful woman in Hollywood, and you don't think that's relevant?" He shook a finger at her. "That's the trouble with you, Claire. You don't think like a reporter."

"I think like a reporter, all right," she said, her cheeks flushing again and her voice rising a notch. "The trouble is, you don't think of me as a reporter."

He didn't have time to deny the undeniable truth of that statement before Lissa, not used to losing an audience, moved to regain their attention by holding up one manicured hand. "Back to the subject, please. What Claire is trying to tell you, Alec, is that she isn't speaking to Miranda."

"You aren't speaking to her?" he asked Claire. "Not the other way around?"

Lissa went on, in a voice fit for narrating the toniest of television documentaries. "Claire's refusal to forgive her is one of the great regrets of Miranda's life. She lost her best friend over some worthless young man. To be more specific, Claire's fiancé."

"You had a fiancé?" It didn't fit the picture Alec had of Claire.

"Claire had a few fiancés," Lissa said.

"He doesn't need to know that," Claire said, as Alec turned to stare at her with renewed interest.

"Claire." Lissa sighed her impatience. "Miranda's book went to number three on the paperback bestseller list before a string of miracle diet books knocked it off. It's not like the whole world doesn't already know."

"I don't know," Alec said. "Enlighten me."

Lissa started to speak, but Claire interrupted her, her voice uncharacteristically steady and strong. "I was sort of engaged a couple of times in high school and college, although I think Missy exaggerates the number in her book. Missy always came up with schemes for getting rid of these guys for me, sometimes by making them fall for her instead, then breaking their hearts. Then I met Scott, and he asked me to marry him." She paused and stared out the window for a second, her eyes centered somewhere far away. "So Missy decided I needed to be rescued from Scott, too, and she scurried off to New York with him. The next thing I know, she's a big star, she's left Scott, and she wants to make up with me."

Intrigued as he was by her story, Alec wanted to know how it tied in with the letter Claire was holding, still taunting him from its shelter in the envelope. When she had finished, he asked, "And so is this a letter from Miranda Craig?"

Lissa took up the narrative again. "Christine Colby is filming a one-hour special on Miranda next weekend, and it's going to be released just in time for Miranda's next picture, *A Woman's Heart*. It's a real you'll-laugh-you'll-cry sort of movie, and so they want to play up this sweet image for Miranda to go with it. They're filming at the house Miranda bought her parents on the lake in Loudon," she said, mentioning a town about twenty-five miles away. "They want her closest family and friends to join her for a weekend there, and share their memories of her. That letter is from Christine Colby's production company, begging Claire to come."

His response was immediate. "I'm coming with you," he told Claire.

He didn't know whether the shocked look on her face was caused by his audacity or by the prospect of spending a weekend with him. Finally she said, "But you don't think I'm actually going?"

"Of course you're going. And I'm going with you. We're writing a story about it." He gave her what he hoped was a good-natured smile. "Well, I'll be writing the story, but you'll help. There may be things she'll say to you that she won't say to me."

Claire was shaking her head. "She won't be saying anything to either of us, because I'm not going. If I were going, I wouldn't take you. And even if you were there, what makes you think she'd talk to you? She's not going to spill her secrets to some reporter I drag along."

"A, I'm an editor." He cleared his throat. "If you don't mind. B, I won't be there as a reporter. I'll be there as your fiancé."

All three of his writers stared at him. Claire and Lissa were openmouthed, and even the unflappable Hank seemed a little shaken. "Don't you see the beauty in this?"

he asked them. They shook their heads in unison. "Have you been engaged since this...um...whatever his name was?"

"Scott," she said. "If it's any of your business."

"So you haven't," he said. "You bring me, your fiancé, to this shindig to show your friend Missy/Miranda that all is forgiven. After all, if she had let you marry that Scott creep, you never would have stumbled on terrific me."

If it wasn't his imagination, the glare she gave him held a tiny bit of admiration. "That's the most despicable thing I've ever heard," she said. "I can't agree to it."

He saw that his ingenious plan had captured Lissa's imagination at least. "Why not?" Lissa asked. "Be a sport."

Claire didn't say anything, merely took the letter back to her desk and stuck it in her purse. Imagining that she was about to crack under their relentless enthusiasm, Alec stepped up his campaign, chatting to Claire as she ignored him.

"Claire, the only good players are team players. I see I was wrong to think you were one. We would have had a lot of fun scooping the daily paper, but since you aren't willing to go that extra distance for us, that isn't going to be possible." He stretched his arms a little, yawning as he did so. "That's the news business. Not much of a way to make a living. It just keeps food on our tables and gives Mick a hole into which to pour his money." Alec peeked at her to see how she was taking his lecture.

"Mick," she said. "Did you ask Mick about my story? The one about how Carbine Industries is illegally dumping toxic waste in South Ridgeville?"

In fact, he'd forgotten all about it, but before he had a chance to confess, she continued, "Harlan Edwards, a community activist—"

"Harlan Edwards is a professional crank," Alec interrupted. "And professional cranks make bad copy."

At that moment, the door to a small room off the side of the office opened and Mick Regan stumbled out. He walked past the group, saying a terse one word, "Lunch," to them as he passed.

"Alec was just quoting you," Hank told him. "Your feelings on career scofflaws."

"One of my better ones," Mick said, his hand on the door.

"I was just telling Alec," Claire said, her voice rising a bit to catch Mick's attention, "I had an interview with Harlan Edwards earlier this morning."

"Was he sober?" Mick asked.

Claire favored him with a slow smile. "That's funny. People always ask me the same thing about you."

Alec sucked his breath in at that, as did Hank and Lissa, but Mick merely laughed and adjusted his hat. "Kid, you'll get some spunk yet. But that doesn't mean you'll be able to build a story off what one crank tells you."

They watched him go out the door and board the elevator. Alec and Hank, both former students of his, looked after him admiringly. "He was a genius in his day," Alec said.

"And what a short twenty-four hours it was," Claire countered, half under her breath. Alec grinned a little before he caught himself.

"Claire, I'm surprised at you," he said. He watched her stuff a paperback in her oversize purse and hoist the bag onto her shoulder. "Where are you going?"

"Lunch."

He stood in front of her, blocking her way. "Not until you give me a decision on this Miranda Craig thing."

She ducked around him, whopping him in his midsection with her purse as she passed. "I gave you a decision," she said. "My decision was no."

Alec, wincing from the hit, made sure he could speak in something lower than a soprano before he addressed Claire again. "Think it over at lunch," he said, as she crossed the room to the stairwell.

"I don't have to," she said. "I'm not changing my mind."

Alec had sent her to microwave oven demonstrations. Future Farmers of America meetings. A recital given by preschoolers who had not quite grasped the musical instruction provided to them. She had gone anywhere, without complaint. Now was a hell of a time to get a backbone.

"Then maybe you shouldn't come back from lunch," he said. "Unless you're ready to say yes to this story."

Hank and Lissa looked up, alarmed. *"Alec,"* Lissa said, glaring at him. "Claire, he doesn't mean it. He used to give me ultimatums like that all the time. You just pretend not to hear them, and he'll figure out they don't work."

Alec turned to her, frowning. "Will you be quiet?" he rasped. When he turned back to the door, Claire was gone. The two reporters stared at him accusingly.

"She'll be back," Alec told Lissa, who ignored him. "Trust me," he told Hank, who clucked his tongue at Alec and resumed typing. "I know psychology," he said to no one in particular.

He walked to his own desk and took out a stack of current magazines and regional newspapers. "I've got all this reading to catch up on," he told them. "So I'm just going to sit here and read, do a little trend-spotting, till Claire comes back."

Lissa flicked off her computer and stood. "I'll leave a note for the cleaning service to dust you off when they come."

"Claire will be back," he said. "She needs this job." Even as he said it, he realized he didn't know if it were true. Finding out about her friendship with Miranda Craig made him realize he didn't know anything about Claire. Nothing except that until a few minutes ago, she had shaken like a leaf every time he spoke to her. He missed that reaction already.

"You're not going to lunch, too, are you?" he asked Lissa.

"People eat, Alec. They don't all live on venom like you do."

"Why didn't you tell me about Claire before? If you knew about the book?"

Lissa shrugged. "Until I read...umm..."

"Until the contents of that letter were accidentally revealed to you," Alec supplied.

"Yes, exactly," Lissa said. "Until then, I didn't have any idea it was the same Claire Morgan. I didn't even know Claire was from here."

"You wouldn't still have your copy, would you?"

"Oh, I don't know," Lissa said, heading out the door for the elevator. "I think I may have left it around here somewhere."

As the doors swished shut behind her, Alec stepped into the hallway and watched the numbers track the elevator's movement, waiting until Lissa had landed safely in the lobby before making a mad dash for her desk.

So MICK THOUGHT she'd get spunk someday, huh? As if spunk were something you could throw into your grocery cart with your yogurt and peanut butter. As though it were a muscle you could develop with exercise, like power abs in ten minutes a day.

She knew it was wrong to be annoyed with Mick. He was basically harmless, famously tactless and spent his days in an ineffectual muddle. But as Alec and Hank often pointed out, somewhere in his brain were the long-buried secrets of a great newspaperman. Lissa had told Claire that Mick had spent years living off stories from his journalistic heyday, but when he'd inherited some money, he'd had enough of the old newsman's fever to buy the equipment from a sinking paper and crank out his own weekly. Making it almost profitable was something else. That was Alec's doing.

Alec. Claire stabbed at a piece of lettuce in her salad, picturing his face. His regrettably handsome face. When he called to offer her the job with the paper, she'd had a clear vision of him, almost like someone was beaming his photograph to her. She'd imagined his thin, ashy hair, his unassuming build, his Adam's apple constantly bobbing up and down. He could have been straight out of central casting, an actor who plays the peevishly sensible fiancé in a romantic comedy, destined to get thrown over by the last scene.

Two days after his phone call, she'd stumbled into the real thing. More specifically, she'd tripped him as he got on the elevator, and she caused him to shut his tie in the door. He was nice enough about it as she blundered through her apologies, but throughout the elevator ride, she'd prayed that she'd never see this man again. There was something about him—his curly black hair, fabulous blue eyes, the way his lean body seemed to fill the whole elevator with his presence. It was the kind of chemistry they posted warning signs about in laboratories. When they'd gotten off the elevator together, she'd hoped he was just a visiting salesman. When she'd asked for Alec Mason and heard him say "I'm Alec," she saw in his eyes that he was as disappointed as she was. Since that first fateful stumble, their nonrelationship had only gotten worse.

She slipped the paperback mystery out of her purse and opened it, noting with pleasure, that the first victim had many of Alec's traits. Arrogance. Looks to kill for.

"Drowning your sorrows in ranch dressing?" Claire looked up to see Lissa take a seat across from her.

"Low-cal buttermilk, actually," she said, closing her book. She liked Lissa in spite of herself, especially since in many ways the other reporter reminded her of Missy. Or Miranda, as she might as well get used to thinking of her. They were both a little shallow, and neither could hold a secret any longer than it took it to go from her ears to her lips. But both of them had some sparkling quality that made it easy to forget how unreliable they were.

Lissa waved the waitress away, and leaned across the table towards Claire. "He's not worth it," Lissa said. "No man is worth all this trouble."

Claire sighed and pushed her half-eaten salad away. "I know. It's ridiculous to go through this. Even if I couldn't get another job with a paper here, I could go back to school, become qualified to do something. And I've always got waitressing experience."

Lissa was staring at her. "Do you think I'm talking about Alec?"

"Aren't you?"

Lissa shook her head. "Of course not. You need this job with Alec. I'm talking about Scott."

If Mick was right, and spunk really was a tangible thing, then hers had been stolen by Scott. If it had existed at all, then it had long ago been hocked in some New York City pawn shop, probably to pay his rent.

Miranda had been the only person who understood how much she loved Scott. Although that had proven to have its disadvantages, the good part of it was that no one else ever thought to mention him. To her other friends and relatives, he blended in with the string of boys Claire didn't marry. Today was the first time anyone had spoken his name to her in a while, and she was flooded with memories.

Their first meeting, in fact, had been too much like her first meeting with Alec. She hadn't shut his tie in an elevator, but she'd exploded a canned cola on his white oxford shirt on the first day of class, managing to get all food and beverages in the classroom banned by the professor. The other students were a little upset, but Scott hadn't minded. Whatever she did only seemed to endear her more to him. Back then, in her early twenties, she'd had the confidence that came with knowing she was loved. Now, at twenty-six, she had the skittishness that came with knowing she'd been dumped and betrayed.

"Claire." Lissa snapped her fingers. "Come out of fantasy land and decide what you're going to do. You cannot let this shallow, arrogant, deceptive scum keep you from participating in one of the singular experiences of your life."

"Scott's not . . ." Claire started to say. "Well, he is, actually, all of those things. But there was more to him than that." There was no way, she knew, that she could communicate his charms to Lissa. How could she describe his killer smile, or the way his eyes used to light up every time he saw her? Considering what he'd done to her, what could she say to redeem him? He indulged all of her whims. He never found anything about her to criticize. He seemed to love her completely right up until the day he left.

"I'm sure he had his good points," Lissa said soothingly, "Before his betrayal of you made you forget them. My point, though, is that you now have an opportunity other people only dream about." At Claire's questioning look, she said, "Okay, let's do this. Imagine you're looking at a group picture from the third grade."

Claire obeyed. She could see them all, lined up on the gym bleachers. Wild print shirts and wide-legged jeans were in style, and half the girls wore their hair like Princess Leia's.

"What were some of their names?" Lissa asked.

"Shelly, Darrell, Starr, Kelly . . ." Her voice trailed off. "What's the point of this?"

"Wherever those kids are, they're telling everyone they know that they went to school with Miranda Craig. In this town right now, someone's claim to fame is that he pulled Miranda's pigtails."

"That would be Joey Bradley," Claire said.

"Right now, old Joey's down at the auto store, bragging about Miranda being his childhood sweetheart. Shelly and Kelly are gossiping about her at the Laundromat. But do they have invitations to this retreat?"

"I see your point," Claire said. "But I can't go. I don't want to see Miranda again."

"You don't have to forgive her for what she did. That's not part of the invitation."

"To tell you the truth," Claire confided. "I don't want to see Scott. It's not like I'm still in love with him, but I just don't want to see him again."

Lissa was shaking her head even before Claire finished. "Scott's not going to be there."

"He was a significant person in her life," Claire said.

"*Not.* Your best friend from first grade to freshman year in college—that's the kind of person who belongs in a tribute to you. Not the guy you left behind when you made it. He'd have lots of lovely things to say for the cameras."

Like Miranda, Lissa had at the core of her personality a hard-as-nails pragmatism and a well-trained eye for the main chance. If Lissa said Miranda wouldn't have asked him, then Claire believed her. Lissa rose, smoothing her linen skirt out as she stood.

"Come on back to work," she told Claire. "Even if you don't change your mind about going to the filming, Alec's not really going to fire you. If he did, you'd just have to go crying to Mick. After all, he's the one who signs the checks."

That, Claire thought, epitomized the difference between them. Lissa was the kind of woman who noticed who signed the checks, while she, Claire, let those details slip by. Maybe it was time to start paying attention.

"Even if you don't want to work for Alec anymore, you're still holding a ticket for an all-expense-paid trip to Miranda Craig's spread. You should use it."

She should use it. As she bid goodbye to Lissa, Claire felt the first shivers of a great idea coming on. She signaled the waitress for more coffee and slipped a notebook out of her purse. She would meet with Alec, but she wouldn't be as unprepared for this encounter as she had been for their first one. This time, she would know what to expect. This time, she had a plan.

2

"I BROUGHT YOU something, Alec." As Lissa dropped a wrapped sandwich on his desk, Alec shoved her purloined copy of the biography in his top desk drawer and hastily picked up the *Wall Street Journal*.

"Lots of interesting human-interest stuff in here today," he told Lissa, unwrapping the layers of aluminum foil and biting into the sandwich, so hungry he didn't care whether it was liverwurst or lean roast beef. "Lots of lifestyle features," he told her, gesturing at the paper. "You should read it sometime."

"Yeah, well, if they come up with a new way to say the bride wore white, be sure and let me know."

Turkey with mustard. A good choice, he thought, as his tastebuds finally identified the meal he was gulping down. "Did you happen to see Claire?"

"She wasn't at the deli," Lissa said, and left it at that. Alec waited at his desk, his whole body tuned to the sounds of the building, waiting for Claire's light step on the stairwell or the ping of the elevator as it rose. He got his hopes up when the elevator stopped at their floor, but it was only Mick, returning from his lunch.

It didn't take Mick long to spot what was wrong with the picture. "Where's Claire?"

"Claire is . . . umm." There was no use lying about it, Alec realized. Lissa would rat on him in a second if he didn't come clean. "We're not exactly sure."

"You didn't fire her, did you?"

"In a manner of speaking, no."

"But in another manner of speaking, maybe?" Mick asked. "You'd better come to my office."

No one ever had the heart to tell Mick that his office was meant to be a utility and supply closet. Extra pens, computer paper and all the other supplies the staff needed had to be stacked in boxes along the floor of the larger office, or hidden in the paper's basement office with the production and four-person advertising staff. Last year, at Christmas, Alec had taken up a collection to put heating and air-conditioning vents in Mick's quarters, but he only had raised enough for a clearance-model ceiling fan. He sat down in one of the room's two chairs and began to fill Mick in, the fan whirring above him noisily as he spoke.

He glossed over the part about how he'd learned what was in Claire's letter, but he could tell that even without hearing about that particular breach of ethics, Mick didn't approve of what he'd done.

"You fired her because she wouldn't take you to a party?" Mick asked him.

That wasn't how he would have put it, but it seemed to be what he'd done. He tried to justify his actions. "It's not that. It's that she had this valuable connection, and she never mentioned it."

Mick seemed puzzled. "I know Miranda Craig is from here, and I know you want to pull one over on the daily, but I just don't see why America's eating her up. She's kind of horse-faced, isn't she?"

Alec sighed. He could feel the day's adrenaline rush seeping out of him, leaving him subdued and depressed. He'd chased a story and lost it. That had never happened before to Alec, and he didn't like the feeling.

"Mick," he said. "Girls look like that now."

"What? You mean like their genes are changing or something? All that radiation we've been fooling around with since the war?'' He shook his head. ''Claire's a hell of a lot prettier, if you ask me.''

Alec stood abruptly. ''I guess I'd better get back to my desk.''

''It's a red-letter day when a man who gets paid for his powers of observation can't see the obvious.''

''Thanks for that vote of confidence,'' Alec said, opening the door.

''Alec.'' He was halted by the unusually firm tone in Mick's voice. ''Sometime, every reporter loses a story he really wants.''

Alec stopped, halted by a vision of the stories he might be tracking if he had remained at the Atlanta paper. That could have led to him becoming the Southeast correspondent for the *New York Times*. Or maybe he would have ended up working for the *Washington Post,* taking an occasional break from investigative reporting to enjoy movies, restaurants and rock bands that would never make it to Ridgeville.

Instead, he'd gambled it all away on the chance to do something worthwhile as the editor of his hometown paper. If the closest thing he could find to something worthwhile was an interview with Miranda Craig, he wasn't going to let it slip out of his hands.

''Not me,'' Alec said. ''Not yet.''

Hank left right at five, his work up to its usual impeccable standards. Lissa left with forty more words to go on her write-up of a fashion show that had taken place at a local tearoom.

''Forty words,'' Alec told her. ''Just put more adjectives in.''

''I've used all the adjectives I know,'' Lissa said. She glanced at her watch. ''You put in your share. Either that or tell production to leave extra spaces between the words.''

Lissa's stories were already set in such large type that they were in danger of looking like society news written for the visually impaired.

"Where do you have to be?" Alec asked.

"I've got a blind date with the law partner son of one of the women I met at the show."

He didn't even try to talk her into staying. Lissa's job took second place to her social climbing, and the fact that the two occupations so often coincided was probably the only thing that kept her there. He had gone out with Lissa in journalism school, until she learned that he wasn't heir to some Mason family fortune. She was the first person he thought of when he needed to hire a society writer, but he wasn't going to be able to keep her forever. She was only honing her skills in the relatively small pond of Ridgeville before taking them to places where the fishing was better. When that happened, he'd have to replace her with someone who was just as eager as she was to claw her way into the lives of the people she wrote about.

That's not Claire, he thought. It didn't matter what she had fought with Miranda about. If Claire had been anyone else, she'd have been so impressed by Miranda's fame and wealth that she would have called her up a long time ago. He'd only skimmed her biography, trying to spot Claire's name, but the gist of the thing was that Miranda had found it to be a cold, cold world once she'd become one of Hollywood's most photographed faces. She wanted to have someone she could trust the way she had trusted Claire.

Mick left just a few minutes after Lissa, and Alec was alone in the office. He knew it was useless to stay a second longer. He no longer believed Claire would come back to work. It was a shame, really. Not only was she the only person willing to drive out to surrounding counties to file stories about two-headed garden snakes and quilting bees, she also wrote the best prose on the paper—excepting his, of course.

He should have left already, but sheer stubbornness was holding him to his desk. He had plenty of work to do—reading over the copy Lissa and Hank had left for him, and drafting commentary for the editorial page, but he couldn't focus on any of it. Annoyed, he took Miranda Craig's book out of the drawer and picked up where he had left off.

Twenty pages later, he heard a half-whispered "Alec?"

The book fell from his hands as he jumped in his seat and looked up to see Claire standing in front of him. "Damn, Claire, don't you knock?"

She pushed her hair behind her ear and crossed her arms over her chest. "I'm sorry I startled you," she said. "I thought that since I work here, it would be okay to walk in without knocking."

Since I work here. His chest flooded with relief at the phrase. He would not have to appease Mick by groveling to get her back. He would not have to search for another reporter willing to take on the homey slice-of-life stories the paper's audience demanded.

"Next time, clear your throat or something."

He picked up the *Wall Street Journal,* which he had already read, and feigned an interest in a story about rising produce prices. Peeking over the edge of the paper, he watched as Claire went to her computer and tapped a few keys. Within a few seconds, paper was spewing out of the laser printer that sat between Hank and Lissa's desks. She collected the sheets, took them back to her desk, slipped them into a file folder and walked back toward him with it. He buried his head in the paper again.

"Can I talk to you for a second?"

He put the paper down. "Look, if it's about what I said…" He was going to say he hadn't really meant it, but Claire stopped him.

"No, it's not about that, exactly, although you were wrong to use threats to get me to agree with your plan."

If it was an apology she was after, she was out of luck. Let her think he was a tough guy. "I was only doing what I thought I had to do to get a story."

Claire nodded. "I understand completely," she said. "Even if you don't think I do." She looked around the room, then asked, "Can I drag a chair over here?"

"Sure."

She scooted a chair in front of his desk, her hair falling around her face as she moved. Once seated, she pushed her hair back over her shoulders and said, "But I was wrong, too, in not realizing how I could use this invitation."

"To take me," he said.

She shook her head. "N-o-o-o," she told him, the syllable a model of verbal hesitation. She drew her hair up with her hands and lifted it off her neck before letting it fall to her shoulders again. Playing with her hair was one of Claire's more pronounced nervous habits. He had never noticed how much it annoyed him.

"Then what?" he asked, exasperated.

"You remember the movie *Willie Wonka?*" she asked him.

He could not afford to lose his temper before he found out what Claire meant to do with that invitation. "Did you review it recently?" he asked helpfully.

"No. From when we were kids," she said. She bent down and retrieved the Miranda Craig biography he had dropped. Placing it on his desk, she said, "You are about my age, aren't you?"

"A year older," he conceded. "I think I remember it. Gene Hackman?"

"Gene *Wilder.* The point is, everyone wants to go to this chocolate factory, but Charlie is one of the few people who has a magic ticket."

"And?"

"I have what basically amounts to a magic ticket. You don't. Now Charlie just wants the experience of going to the factory, even though he does wind up running it, eventually, because he's pure of heart."

Claire had taken their fight much harder than he expected. She had fallen off the deep end. "You know," he told her kindly, "I don't remember the movie very well, but I wouldn't draw too close a comparison between you and Charlie."

"What I'm trying to tell you," she said, leaning across his desk, only inches away from him, "is that just like Charlie got what he wanted from his ticket, I'm going to get what I want from mine."

She was so close to him that he could smell her hair. A peculiarly seductive scent that resulted when the odor of a neighborhood greasy spoon mingled with the honey-suckle of shampoo. "What do you want?" Alec asked. He held his breath as he waited for the answer.

She relinquished the folder she'd been clutching, and placed it on top of his desk. "I want my story about South Ridgeville in the paper...."

"Claire..."

"Plus a couple of more real news stories."

He gestured to the folder. "This is something about South Ridgeville?"

"It's a draft of my notes and some interview transcripts just to give you a feel for what I'm doing. Yes, you'll find quotes from Harlan Edwards, a professional crank who hits the whiskey a little too hard sometimes, but you'll also find other people. People who want the whole community to know that Carbine Industries is treating one of their city's neighborhoods as a wastebin for hazardous material."

It would never work. "Claire, you're a good writer—"

"Thank you," she interrupted.

"But," he said, letting the conjunction hang in the air. "That's not the same thing as being a good reporter."

She opened her mouth, then shut it again. He continued. "When you first start out, every story looks like a Pulitzer winner. In a big city, sometimes your hunch is true. But in a medium market like Ridgeville, you start realizing you aren't going to get many big stories. Then you begin to notice that the same people, people like Harlan Edwards, are always trying to get you riled about something. It just becomes noise after a while."

"So you'd rather sit at your desk and rewrite the press releases the local bigwigs send you."

"Look." His tone was sharp. "Even if I thought this was a good idea, Mick would think otherwise. You know he's got final veto. I couldn't get this past him."

"You have to," she said simply. "If you want to go to the Craigs' with me, then you have to convince Mick that this is a timely and important piece, and that you can't wait for me to start work on it. Then you'll have to repeat that process with several more stories of my choosing."

He thought for a second. "Two more," he said. "That's several."

"Four," she said, "is closer to the true meaning of the word."

He opened his mouth to say he couldn't be blackmailed in this way, but before he could speak, he was overcome, imagining Miranda down by the lake with him. She was confiding her most intimate thoughts and fears to him—for attribution.

What did he have to lose in exchange? He could give Claire the go-ahead on her articles, but what was to stop him from scheming with the production manager to bury them all on the back page? And once Claire realized that all there was to her toxic dumping story was Harlan Edwards making his usual big deal about nothing, she'd realize she didn't have what it took to run with the big boys. She'd come crawling with her apologies to him.

"It's a deal," he said. Then it hit him that there might be another problem. "Does she know that you're a reporter?" he asked Claire, with concern in his voice. "I mean, that's not going to make her take back her offer, is it?"

"Oh, no," Claire said. "Before I got the job here, when I was doing some free-lance work, she offered to give me an interview that I could sell to the paper or magazine of my choice. Penance, you know, for what she did."

"You turned her offer down?"

The smile she gave him was an inscrutable one. "I already know what Miranda Craig's favorite color is. I wouldn't need her permission to sell my memories of her."

She stood, then walked over to her desk and turned her computer off. As he opened his mouth to ask her another question, she said, "Purple."

"Purple," he repeated. He said, mostly to himself, "I imagine purple flowers would look good against her blond hair."

Claire gave him an amused stare. "Alec, don't forget your brilliant scheme. You're going there as my fiancé, remember?"

His reply, cutting as it was, tumbled out before he could stop it. "Yeah? Well, maybe she'll see fit to steal me, too."

He wished immediately that he could take back what he'd said, but Claire only smiled. "Sticks and stones, Alec."

Their agreement hadn't even been in effect for a half hour, and he already wanted to strangle her. "I know. You're the one holding the ticket to the chocolate factory." He jumped up and grabbed his briefcase, holding the door open for Claire as the two of them left the office. "I'll walk you to your car. I don't want anything to happen to you before next weekend." Nothing, but nothing, was going to keep this starving man from his trip to the candy store.

"HAVE FUN EATING prime rib in the country moonlight while I'm sweating over a barbecue pit or aching in my high heels," Lissa told Alec, trying to put into her tone just the right mix of hurt and righteous indignation. Alec never looked up.

"I will. Thanks." He frowned at his computer, then typed something in with two fingers.

Lissa put her hand on her hip, annoyed. That voice had never failed to work for her before. Alec might play tough, but she knew he could only hear a few sentences in that decibel range before he cracked.

"I said don't even think about me when you're exploiting Claire for your own selfish purposes. The poor girl is trembling at the thought of facing her painful past, but you don't care, just as long as you get your story."

Alec ignored her, but Hank spoke up, as if by proxy. "Yesterday, you thought this was a good idea."

True, she thought. But yesterday, she had been star struck at the thought of an exclusive Hollywood soiree taking place in the hills of east Tennessee. Not until later had it occurred to her that she wasn't going.

"It's just that I didn't dream that I would be stuck with so much extra work." She gestured to her desk, covered almost exclusively by tabloids and fashion magazines, but covered, nonetheless. She sighed loudly and dramatically. "A profile of some goofy professor, two extra wedding write-ups and the best barbecue contest."

"You don't have to tell me your work load," Alec said, twisting his tie a little. "Remember I assigned it to you?" His voice had no hint of friendliness. "So how about stretching your mind past the few adjectives you know and giving me an honest day's work, okay?''

"You don't have to yell," Lissa said.

"Don't yell at her," Claire said, walking in and putting her bag down on her desk.

"You're late," Alec snapped.

Lissa was about to speak up on her behalf when Claire gazed at Alec coolly and said, "I was in front of the building by nine, but the horrible timbre of your tone made the building shake. I thought it best to proceed with caution."

Well, well, Lissa thought. Just maybe Claire was going to be okay after all.

Claire turned toward Lissa. "I heard what you said about the extra work, and I don't think it's fair. I'll go ahead and do an extra movie review, plus the professor, before I leave. I've also got a lead on a guy who has a country music museum in the basement of his house, and I'll give him a call."

"Thank you, Claire. That's sweet."

Alec pulled the assignment sheet from a clipboard on his desk. "Okay, listen up everybody. Claire, for no good reason, has let Lissa off the hook, and Hank's taking a couple of the stories I would normally do. We come back on Monday..." Mute agreement seemed to be all he required of the staff, and Lissa tuned him out until she heard him say, "And Mick's going to cover that city council meeting."

"What did you say?" Lissa and Claire spoke at once.

"Mick is covering a city council meeting," he repeated.

Like Alec, Hank was always quick to rush to Mick's defense. "It isn't the end of civilization," he interrupted.

"It's got to be the end of the paper," Lissa said.

"Alec, maybe this isn't such a great idea," Claire told him. "Maybe I should just go to Miranda's and tell you about it."

Alec was slowly turning a dull, dusky red. His jaw clenched, he said, "Mick..."

"Is he here?" Claire looked at his office with alarm.

"Are you kidding?" Lissa asked. "It isn't noon yet."

"As I was saying." There was a dangerous edge to Alec's voice. "About Mick. Mick was the kind of journalist who could decimate politicians with just a few choice sentences. Mick was the kind of journalist who could smell corruption and greed from miles away. So I have complete faith in his ability to sit in a room and write down what he hears around him. I want to write about Miranda Craig. I'm going to write about Miranda Craig. And I know that when I leave, I'm leaving the paper in Mick's more than capable hands." He pointed at Claire. "You called to confirm that you were coming, right?"

Lissa noticed that Claire didn't lose as much color as she once did whenever Alec talked to her that way. "I'm sorry. I forgot." She dug the letter out of her purse and dialed. Although Hank went on working, Lissa saw that Alec, like herself, wasn't trying to hide the fact that he was eavesdropping.

Claire went through the basics of the trip with someone at Christine's office. As it seemed she was about to hang up, Alec waved his hand and pointed to his chest.

Claire, looking puzzled, merely shrugged at him. Alec dove for a piece of paper on Lissa's desk and scrawled "Taking me" across it. He held it up.

"I forgot to tell you. I plan to bring my fiancé. Do I need to clear that with you?"

Lissa watched with interest as Claire's cheeks flushed and her lips tightened. "I appreciate your concern," she said. "But this is a fiancé of a different sort."

She hung up and turned to her desk, her back to the rest of them. Lissa put her finger on her lips, gesturing for Alec to be quiet, but he said, "So what's the deal? Can I go or not?"

"I've got to call Miranda's mom." She pulled out a tattered maroon address book and began flipping through it.

Painful as it might be for her, it was time to help Claire face facts.

"You know, Claire," Lissa said, studying her manicure as she spoke. "I just realized it might strike someone as odd that you're introducing Alec to Miranda."

Claire seemed genuinely puzzled. "Odd how?"

"If you really cared about him, I wouldn't think you would bring him anywhere near her."

"I don't think so, Lissa." Claire's denial seemed sincere. "I think if I really cared about him, I'd trust him so absolutely that I wouldn't mind if he were introduced to other women."

Alec cleared his throat. "Could you stop talking about me like I'm the teenaged bride in an arranged marriage?"

The two women ignored him. "Whatever you say," Lissa told her. "But don't be surprised if she asks you about it."

Claire made the connection quickly, and Lissa nonchalantly flipped through a magazine while she waited for the small talk to pass. Claire missed Mrs. Craig's cornbread, yack yack yack. She was so excited to be able to see the new house, yack yack yack. Lissa stifled a yawn.

She put the magazine down when Claire finally broached the subject of Alec, literally squirming as she lied to the woman. Lissa was just glad Mrs. Craig couldn't see Claire's guilty expression.

"How's it going?" Lissa mouthed. She didn't have to wait very long for an answer. Claire listened intently for a moment, then gulped a little, her cheeks reddening again and that same grim expression taking over.

"No, Barbara, I know that she's not the sort of person who acts out of malice. Whatever she's done she's done out of her incredible spontaneity."

Oh, really. Surely the old lady wasn't going to fall for that. She must have, though, because Claire was once again on the listening end of the conversation.

"Barbara, I know what you're trying to say."

Uh-huh, Lissa thought. I bet I do, too.

Claire let out a kind of strangled laugh. "I don't have any worries in that department. I mean, he seems like the most wonderful man in the world to me, but what would Miranda want with him?"

Alec's expression darkened, and he stomped back to his desk. He left before he could see the expression Lissa caught as Claire looked toward the ground and said into the phone, "No, you're right. Scott was no prize, either, was he? No, Barbara, I wasn't worried about him—I knew all along he wouldn't be there."

There was eavesdropping, and then there was making a spectacle out of someone's psychic pain. Having none of her own, and wanting to keep it that way, Lissa stopped paying attention to Claire's increasingly despondent tone and turned her computer on for the first time that morning.

She looked up again when she heard Alec say, "Hey, Claire. Thanks for making me sound like Clark Kent."

Claire said nothing, only went to her computer, turned it on and began typing in that same mindlessly dedicated way she always did.

"So what's the deal?" Alec asked. "Can I go or not?"

"You can go." At Claire's distressed tone, Lissa looked up to see someone who was about to go on an all-out crying jag. Her eyes were blinking rapidly behind her glasses, her nose looked like she'd been out on an all-night drinking binge and her voice was cracking. Lissa was about to offer a sympathetic word or two when Claire bolted out of her chair and ran for the stairwell. To the ladies' room, no doubt.

Alec stared after her. "Can you explain that to me?" he asked Lissa.

"Not so you'd understand," she said sarcastically, and continued her one-word-per-minute typing routine. The slow pace of her work left her with plenty of time to think about other things. Plenty of time to think of a way to help out poor Claire.

3

"YOU DON'T KNOW what I would do to have this hair," Claire's friend Allie told her as she whipped a wide-toothed comb through Claire's brown locks. "It's thick, it's heavy. There's a lot of it. You could work hair like this." Allie and Claire had been having this argument since high school. Then, as now, Claire simply ignored her.

She didn't know what she was doing at Allie's Designs of Your Life Hair Studio anyway, not when tomorrow was *The Day*. Whatever she could do for her looks tonight was not going to rival the kind of beauty support team Miranda was sure to have working for her. Changing her looks would only make Alec think she was insecure about this trip. Unless he didn't notice at all. Now there was a comforting thought.

Growing up, people had always defined Miranda and Claire by their differences. Claire was the quiet one, Miranda the outgoing one. Claire smart, Miranda funny. She winced when she thought of the other distinction. Back then, Miranda was referred to as the tomboy, and Claire was the pretty one.

The same people who'd once said it was lucky that the awkwardly teenage Miranda had such a fun personality were now falling all over themselves to say they always knew what a beauty she'd grow up to be. Grateful that people had finally stopped comparing her to Miranda, Claire never paid any attention to her appearance at all, except for availing herself of the opportunity to blend in with the walls whenever possible. She knew that drove Allie crazy.

"It's not enough to keep your hair clean, Claire," Allie said. "You need a style."

Claire made a face at her in the mirror. Allie's idea of a hairstyle inevitably involved hot rollers, cases of hair spray and at least two hours of labor each morning. No thanks.

"I have bangs," she said.

"Bangs are not a style."

"I can't fit complicated hair into my life," she said, as the stylist snipped her split ends with an expert hand.

Allie snorted. "I know what your life involves, Claire. Going to movies by yourself and sitting at home writing. You could hang out in curlers all day and no one would notice."

"Thanks," Claire said. It was true that she'd spent as little time in the office as possible this week, trying to avoid Alec. Since she'd stood up to him about the invitation, she hadn't exactly been the same quivering mass of jelly he knew and disdained. It would be great if she could keep up the act, but she didn't trust her new composure. Look at that embarrassing minibreakdown she'd had after talking to Barbara Craig. She didn't want to be in the middle of some brave speech to Alec, then start to stammer and stumble at the crucial point.

Allie looked at her with a critical eye. "At least let's give your hair a little color. Something that will bring out the copper glints that are already there."

Claire lifted a lock of hair and looked at it. "I'm just grateful it isn't gray."

"Gray hair should be the least of your worries," Allie said in the conspiratorial stage whisper she used before she launched into an especially choice piece of gossip. "I heard that Miranda got so stressed out on the set of her last movie that her hair fell out and she had to use falls."

"Where did you hear that?" Claire asked.

"From her cousin, Chris. I saw him at the grocery store."

She should have guessed. Every time Claire ran into Chris, he had a new revelation. "I'm surprised anyone buys those gossip mags at all," Claire said. "With him stationed by the impulse rack, waiting to tell people what he's already spilled to them."

Allie acted as though she didn't hear her. "He also said she's throwing this big Miranda lovefest on the lake, for her friends and family, and that Christine Colby is going to film and air the thing. She's invited a bunch of people there to say how wonderful she is for the cameras."

Claire shifted uncomfortably in her seat. "That sounds interesting," she said. But even though she'd successfully fibbed to Barbara Craig days before, that had been over the telephone, and Barbara's limited skill for seeking out scandal was no match for Allie's.

"You're going, aren't you? That's why you made this appointment." Claire nodded. "If I have to handcuff you to this chair with spiral rollers, you're getting some red in your hair."

Allie had to be filled in on all the details of the trip. Although she and Claire had been close friends in high school, she and Miranda had never gotten along, probably because it was hard for two people to share center stage gracefully. As Claire told Allie the story of the invitation, she realized how ridiculous it all sounded. Allie, in her inimitable way, got straight to the heart of it.

"You have a crush on this guy, don't you?" she asked.

Claire balked at such a mundane characterization. "No, I don't have a crush on him. In fact, I feel kind of ill and disoriented whenever he's around."

"Claire, honey, *that is a crush.* You're out of practice, girl." The color rinse was finished, and Allie handed Claire a magazine to read while she sat and waited for her hair to dry. She sat down in the chair next to Claire. "Is he very cute?"

"The poison in his soul far outweighs his outside attractiveness," Claire said.

"Very cute, then," Allie said. "And is he seeing anyone?"

Claire had to plead ignorance. "I don't know. I don't know anything about his personal life besides the fact that he can't tolerate me. The other woman who works there, Lissa, once hinted to me that they went out when they were in college."

"Lots of people go out, Claire. They go out on one or two dates, but they don't feel the need to pursue it any further. Most women don't consider getting hitched to every man who rings the doorbell."

"Neither do I, anymore." Starting tomorrow, she'd be called upon to tell lie after lie, beginning with her and Alec being a couple and continuing on through the moment she pretended to forgive Miranda her trespasses. But she wasn't lying about what she told Allie. She was too old to keep going out with guys she couldn't stand just because she couldn't break it to them that she wasn't interested. Better to make sure they didn't notice her at all. And as for the kind of engagement she'd had with Scott—well, she never wanted to give her heart away like that again.

"Do you want my advice?" Allie asked.

"Tell me how I could stop you from giving it to me."

"I think you should take your new hair and new wardrobe up to the Craigs and enjoy yourself like there's no tomorrow. Eat great food, drink great wine—oh, wait, the Craigs don't drink—okay, smuggle in great wine, and let their servants wait on you hand and foot."

Allie had painted a tempting picture, but Claire was hung up on one of the details. "I didn't buy a new wardrobe."

"Not yet." Allie pointed to the large clock on the wall to the right of Claire. "You're my last client. When we get out of here, we're going shopping."

"I have clothes, Allie. I'm already packed."

Allie put her finger on her chin in an exaggerated motion. "Let me guess what you consider clothes for the weekend. You were going to pack that midcalf navy skirt you wore to my great-aunt's funeral, the designer dress you got on clearance even though it's a little irregular, your faded baggy jeans and that huge white shirt you stole from Scott. To top it all off, a bathing suit with a skirt attached to it, probably one your mother gave you because she considered it too old for her."

"They're back in style," Claire said.

"For people who are planning to time-travel back to the turn of the century," Allie said. "Look at me." Claire obeyed. "I look good. But what you see here is work. You've seen me without my makeup, or trying to get my hair to hold a curl. Now I look at you and I say, "Gee, Claire's got great hair, beautiful big eyes, a body Marilyn Monroe herself might have envied, and what is she doing with it? Hiding it all.""

Claire pretended to read the poster-sized advertisements hung around the room, but Allie went on. "So I ask myself why? Now in high school, Claire might have lost her mascara tube a few times at the bottom of her grocery sack of a purse, and she didn't always have time to brush her hair thoroughly before class, but at least she wore clothes that fit. She didn't try to hide how pretty she was. So do you know what I think?"

Claire didn't answer.

"I think you don't want anyone to know you're attractive. You're terrified that some man will find out how cute and smart and funny you really are, and fall in love with you again." She shook her head. "I've seen your type on 'Oprah.'"

Claire dismissed Allie's rant, trying not to dwell on whether or not it was true. "All this free analysis just because I won't go shopping with you?"

Allie put her brush down and looked Claire straight in the eye. "I'm not going to let you go to Miranda's looking like some low self-esteem poster child. Look—do you act this shy when you go out on stories?"

"I never get to go out on real stories, probably because Alec thinks I'm too quiet. But in the one I've been working on, no, I haven't been shy."

"How do you get past it?"

Claire blushed, realizing that what she was about to say might sound silly to her friend. "I pretend I'm a hardhitting, tough-as-nails kind of girl reporter. Sort of like Rosalind Russell in *His Girl Friday*."

Allie was nodding. "So for this weekend, what you do is decide to play the part of self-confident, attractively dressed, assertive young woman. Let that character deal with Miranda and Alec. That's all you have to do. We'll go get your costume right now."

Claire gave her a dubious look, and Allie said, "Don't worry. We'll find some compromises between my tastes and yours."

Claire knew what that meant. Whatever else she came home with, you could bet that at least one of the items would be scarlet and cut to there.

GIRL DIRECTIONS. He should have known that's what Claire was giving him when he talked to her on the phone the night before. Girl directions relied on landmarks rather than on exact distances, especially if they were landmarks that no longer existed. He, for example, was supposed to look for Mr. Turner's store on the right, although Claire said Mr. Turner had been dead for almost twenty years and the store, after a number of fly-by-night owners, was now operated by some Yuppie upstarts. Her phrase, not his.

There it was on his right—Gorgonzola and Pine Nuts On Sale, This Week Only.

Girl directions were also marked by a stubborn refusal to use the interstate for its intended purpose—to get from one part of the city to another. So it was that Alec, having spent his morning on the windy, twisting back roads heading into the western part of the county, stuck behind a tractor at one point and stopped by a herd of cows at another, found that the road Claire lived on was just a short hop from an interstate exit, near where their publisher, Mick, lived. He crumpled up the directions he'd scribbled down, and turned left.

Far be it from Claire to know exactly how far down the road she lived, although she had guessed it was about three miles. Instead, she had given him the names of subdivisions, and he grew increasingly uncomfortable as he eyed the minimansions in Belle Meade Estates, Knottingwood Forest and Riversound. Riversound? Hey, people, it's a lake, he thought to himself. A fairly boring one at that. Still, waterfront property was waterfront property, and he wondered how Claire could afford to have a house out here. Miranda's book hadn't said Claire was rich.

She wasn't. As he took the gravel road right past the entrance to Westchester Court—"across from what used to be a huge ditch, but then some teenager fell in and they filled it, even though he was okay"—he saw a small frame bungalow at the top of the hill. He rolled up the driveway, his tires crunching on the rocks, and parked next to the house. Before he went to the door, he wanted to confirm a suspicion he had. He started to climb on his car, but then considered his new wax job. Instead, he sized up a tree at the back of the house and shimmied up it, careful not to rip his khakis as he did so. Peering through the branches, he could see a few rickety old buildings to his left, along with what looked to be the crumbling foundation of a house. At the bottom of the hill was the lake. Just as he'd thought. You could fit a whole subdivision on Claire's property—two, if people didn't mind their neighbors saying "Bless you" when they sneezed inside their own homes. All that property, all that water, and all of it wasted on the impractical Claire.

"What are you doing in my tree? Making sure you weren't followed by a rival reporter?"

A muffled curse escaped his lips as he hit his head on the branch above him. Clutching his head with one hand, he lowered himself down to the ground with the other, and found himself face-to-face with Claire. At least, he thought it was Claire. There was a resemblance in the face, sure, but her wide amber eyes were highlighted against her pale skin, and her lips and cheeks were bright and—there was no other word for it—inviting. Her hair waved out over her shoulders, and the sun captured its copper glints. Alec caught himself staring at the simple white dress that hugged her chest, shimmered over her hips and halted unexpectedly at midthigh.

Unbusinesslike thoughts were racing through his head, but he managed to refrain from saying any of them. Instead, he settled on, "You're wearing that?"

Her mouth twisted into the frown he knew she reserved for him alone. It was Claire, all right. "What's wrong with it?"

Nothing was wrong with it. That was precisely the trouble. "It's so . . ."

"So . . . ? So what exactly? Come on, Alec. You know lots of adjectives." She crossed her arms. "Would you like to borrow a thesaurus?"

He changed the subject back to one that put him in a more favorable light. "I would have been here a lot sooner, except that your directions took me past every roadside stand and home-based flea market in the county. I don't know why you didn't tell me your house was just off of Exit 10."

Claire was walking back toward the house, and he scrambled to catch up. As she held the screen door for him, she said, "There's more to see if you travel the back roads. The interstate's so boring, don't you think?"

"Efficient. That's the adjective for the interstate," he said. As Claire disappeared from the living room into a hallway, he surveyed what he could see of the small house. The kitchen was a cluttered and funky area filled with older-model appliances and knickknacks straight out of the 1950s. Yellow linoleum flooring gave way to hard wood to mark where the kitchen ended and the living/dining room began. Books were stacked all over the dining room table, and magazines were nestled among the pillows on the faded pin-striped sofa. The refinished wood was partly covered by a comfortable cotton rug. The framed prints hanging on the walls—Edward Hopper and a few artists he didn't recognize—lent a quirkiness to the homey feel of the place.

He was going through her bookshelves when Claire came back into the room, hauling one, two, three suitcases behind her.

"You're only going to be gone three nights," he said. "You wear a suitcase full of clothes everyday?"

"I was a Girl Scout," she said. "I'm always prepared."

He grabbed two of the suitcases and took them to his car, Claire following him with the last one. "It's the Boy Scouts who are prepared, remember? Of which I was one. I only have one suitcase and the bag my computer gear is in."

She didn't answer him, simply walked back into the house. "I have to make sure I didn't forget anything," she told him. She peered at the on/off switches of each appliance. "So, anyway, you never told me what you were doing in my tree."

This was something he had only recently noticed about Claire. When she asked something, she never let it rest until she got the answer she wanted, like that thing about whether or not XYZ corporation was doing whatever in south Ridgeville. Normally, he would have said such persistence was the sign of a good reporter. In her case, he chalked it up to Claire's being stubborn.

"I was ... uh ... looking to see if your house was on the lake. I noticed there was a lake out here. Umm... Boy, that must be fun for you, huh?" Was it his imagination, or was he stammering? He had never heard caution or unease in his voice before. He'd only been in Claire's house five minutes, and he was already acting like her.

"Why didn't you ask me if I lived on the lake? Or even walk down the hill and see?"

"I was being sort of ... well, not secretive, but ..." His voice trailed off.

Her remark was almost too quiet to hear. "Yeah, you were real inconspicuous up in that oak."

"I'm sorry. What did you say?" He pointed to his right ear. "I played guitar in a band in college, and it left me with a slight hearing problem."

"That's too bad," Claire said. "If you need any help eavesdropping this weekend, let me know." She cut off the drip in her sink faucet, and closed and locked the kitchen window. "I've got to make sure I turned off the TV in my room," she said. "Be right back."

When she returned, carrying her purse, he said, "I guess you get really tired of people telling you how much money you could make by selling this land."

She fished an earring out of her purse and put it on, then found the other one. "Everyone who knows me knows that's a useless conversation."

"I bet your neighbors don't think so." He hadn't meant to get into this topic at all, but her amused expression spurred him on. "I'd say they think that since the demographics of this area have changed, that it really isn't fair for one person to be able to buck that tide."

"Wait a minute," she said. As soon as he heard the indignation in her voice, he remembered the passion she'd brought to her argument about going to Miranda's. "My grandparents, and their grandparents, lived out here way before it was fashionable. They were farmers, and this was considered the sticks. No one wanted to drive out this far. But now that people are so accustomed to zipping along the interstate in their BMWs and—" she looked out the window at his car "—Hondas, they think they should have all the prime real estate. Well, I think it's okay if I hold on to this land."

"Where would the country be if everyone had that attitude about progress?" he asked her. As soon as he'd said it, he knew he'd lost.

"I guess it would still be in the hands of the Native Americans, wouldn't it?" she said sweetly.

He looked at his watch. "Miss Hollywood's going to think you chickened out on bringing your fiancé. We'd better get moving." He watched as she turned the key in the dead bolt and gave the door a good hard shake.

"I guess that's it," she said. She looked all too confident and cheery. He stopped her as she got into the car. "By the way, Claire. That tree in your backyard? It's a maple. If I were you, I'd call your old Girl Scout leader. I don't think your parents got their money's worth out of the organization."

"DAY ONE WITHOUT our leader. Will we be able to pull together as a team? Or will we give in to laxness and ennui? The heart and soul of the newspaper depend on the two writers seated here," Hank said as he stood in front of Lissa's desk looking down at her.

Lissa scanned her desk for the nearest unbreakable, nonlethal object to toss at Hank. It was a pencil. "Will you quit it already with the bad 'Twilight Zone' imitation? I have a lot on my mind today without being plagued by you."

Catching the pencil in one hand, Hank went back to work, and Lissa curled up in her seat, trying to make herself comfortable.

She was lost in her daydreams, this close to drifting off into a tempting catnap when Hank asked, "Like what?"

Lissa jerked her head up. "Like a lot on my mind."

"For instance."

"For instance, I'm wondering how to cover that barbecue cook-off tonight. I'm now a vegetarian."

"Since when?" Hank asked.

Lissa crumpled up the bag that had held that morning's grilled chicken and biscuit. "Since breakfast."

"Since you've already broken your vows today, you should become one tomorrow, after the story's done."

Hank sounded too much like Alec when he said things like that. This was something Lissa was going to have to nip in the bud, or today and Monday were going to be unbearable. "To borrow a quaint phrase you may remember from your childhood, you are not the boss of me. This just came to me, right after breakfast, as something I had to do. I'm not the kind of woman who puts idealism on hold." She shrugged. "Maybe it's Claire's influence. She's a vegetarian."

Hank busied himself looking for something on his desk. "Yes, but Claire lacks a lot of your more carnivorous aspects."

"Well, her life would be a lot different if she knew how to get her claws out every once in a while."

Hank's disdain for gossip was notorious, so Lissa was surprised when he said, "How so?"

"How so what?"

"How would her life be different?"

She wanted to comment about his new interest in his co-workers' personal lives, but the office was a barren and empty place today, and she couldn't afford to alienate her one hope for conversation. She began to share her theories about Claire.

"If she had gone up to New York to try to get Scott back from Miranda, he would have come back. Just from reading between the lines in that book, I can tell that Scott and Miranda knew they'd made a mistake. They were probably praying for Claire to give them an excuse to break up. But because she gave up, she lost him."

Hank had been typing away at his computer while she talked, but when she finished, he looked up and said, "Maybe she was relieved."

Lissa shook her head. "Didn't you see that faraway look in her eyes when his name came up the other day? Then she practically burst into tears when she talked to Miranda's mother about him."

"I wasn't paying attention."

He was a promising student, Lissa thought, but he was going to have to have a lot more practice at this. "She still loves him. I've been trying to think of a way to help her get on with her life, but I'm clueless. Short of getting Scott back, I don't know what's going to do it."

As soon as she'd said it, she looked at Hank, who met her gaze with some alarm. "I can't believe I know what you're thinking," he said. "But no, you can't. It's impossible, immoral and it will ruin Alec's story."

"It isn't impossible. I bet I could find Scott without much trouble at all. And it would make Claire happy. Anyway, by the time he gets there, Alec should have his story already."

"What about Alec and Claire?" Hank asked.

Lissa waved a hand at him. "We can work around this phony engagement thing. Don't worry about that."

"What if it isn't as phony as we think? Not the engagement, I mean, but the two of them. You know."

Let a man think he understands a little bit about human behavior, and all of the sudden he's declaring himself an expert on the subject. "There is nothing going on between them," Lissa said.

"What makes you so sure?"

Slowly, patiently, as though she were explaining the birds and the bees to someone very young, Lissa tried to tell him why Claire and Alec could never be a couple. "There are two kinds of people in this world. Fling people, and commitment people. Commitment people are the kind who wind up getting engaged to almost everyone they date—like Claire. Fling people can go out a lot, but never have a serious relationship—like Alec."

"You don't think the two can ever be happy?"

"Rarely," Lissa said. "And certainly not in the case of Claire and Alec, all other differences aside. That would be like you and..." She started to say, "and me," but she didn't want to give him any ideas. Instead she said, "Miranda."

"Don't ask me for help," Hank said, turning back to his work.

"I won't need it," Lissa said. She got straight to work, took a sheet of paper out of her desk and wrote "Find Scott" on it. There, that was a start. She underlined the phrase. Scott... Scott who? She opened up her desk drawer, hoping Alec had replaced her copy of the Miranda Craig biography, but it wasn't there. She went to his desk and rifled through the drawers, but didn't see it there, either. Now how was she supposed to find out Scott's last name?

"I need your help," she told Hank.

"I'm not aiding and abetting this crime you're trying to pass off as an act of friendship," he said.

"Don't be melodramatic." Lissa relished being able to say that to someone else. "You know that seminar we were supposed to go to, the one where we learned how to do research from data bases? Remember how I met that cute stockbroker at registration and never quite made it there? Well, now I need to know how to find something.''

Everyone had a weak spot. As she'd hoped, Hank wasn't able to resist an appeal to his skills and his knowledge, and he turned over his terminal. Caught up in the challenge of tracking down the information, he seemed to forget his concerns about the wisdom of what she was doing. Fortunately, Lissa remembered the year Miranda dropped Scott, and they were able to locate stories about her using that date and Scott's first name.

Hank called up a full-text version of one of the stories. Lissa, reading over his shoulder, stopped when she came to the flagged term ''Scott.''

''Scott Granville,'' she read. ''I remember that now.''

With a few expert maneuvers, Hank got out of the data base. ''Of course you remember, now that we've spent all this time on a fifty-dollar-an-hour data base.''

''It's for a good cause,'' Lissa said. ''Now what do I do?''

Hank sighed. ''Do you think he still lives in New York City?'' At her nod, he suggested she try directory assistance. ''I doubt he'll be listed, though. If I were Miranda Craig's ex, I wouldn't be.''

''Don't you see? That's exactly the reason I'm going to find him waiting by the phone.''

And he was. Picking up after one and a half rings, Scott seemed eager to listen to Lissa's spiel. Quickly she explained who she was and how she knew Claire. Then she went for the zinger, telling him how glad she was she caught him before he left for the retreat.

''Claire and our editor are going to be interviewing the attendees there, but I'm trying to get a few comments from people before they go, you know, in case they can't talk freely once they arrive,'' she said.

He was quiet for a second. "Retreat? This is the first I've heard about it."

Lissa feigned shock. "You aren't invited? But you're such an integral part of Miranda's history. You're the authority on that whole struggling actress era of her life." She sighed. "Please say you aren't mad at me for calling you and unearthing all this painful old history. I never dreamed you weren't invited." She went for the clincher. "I know for a fact that Claire expected you to be there."

Hank went into a hysterical coughing fit. Scowling, Lissa put her fingers on her lips and mimed cutting her throat.

"She did? And she was still going to go?" Scott said after a long pause.

"Yes," Lissa lied. "I think she was looking forward to seeing how you'd changed."

"I've changed for the better," he said. She found herself kind of touched by his boyish tone. "I'm not the same guy who ran off with Miranda."

"I'm sure Claire would like to hear that. If only you were going to be there."

Across the telephone wires, she could practically see the little cogs in his brain whirling. "You know, there's got to be some way I can go. If I crash the thing, the worst Miranda can do is throw me out. And that's going to look kind of bad for her, especially if she knows there's a reporter there."

"There you go," Lissa said. "I don't know how long it's been since you've been back here, but if you're serious about coming, they have one-stop flights from New York City to Ridgeville. Getting here would be no trouble at all. I'd be more than happy to pick you up at the airport and give you a ride out there, so you don't have to rent a car." She remembered that she was supposed to be a part of the paper's story. "That would give me a chance to get some quotes from you along the way."

"Lissa, you're great," he said in a warm voice.

They agreed that he would call her when he'd made arrangements for his flight, and she reeled off her home number to him. They said their goodbyes and, satisfied, she hung up the phone and beamed at Hank.

He was plainly less than impressed. "Rhetorical question," he said. "What kind of man flies hundreds of miles to crash a party?"

"One who's desperate for revenge or hopelessly in love." Lissa got her purse from the bottom drawer of her desk. "Both, I bet."

"Where are you going?"

"I'm going to pick up Scott."

"He hasn't even booked a flight yet," Hank said.

"I want to be ready when he calls." She pointed to her rayon skirt and casual blouse. "I'm not driving to the Craig home looking like this."

"What about your stories?"

"I'm sure I'll be back in plenty of time to finish them. But just in case, let me tell you where some of this stuff is." She pointed to a stack of press releases on her desk. "The information about the barbecue contest is somewhere in the pile. It's at seven, but don't feel like you have to stay for very long. You don't even have to hang around for the end of the contest—just ask one of the judges to call you." She dug in her purse for a piece of paper. "Here's the rough draft of that wedding story I was supposed to be writing. Mick was there, since he's friends of the bride's parents, but don't expect him to remember anything about it. I seem to remember there was some ruckus by the punch bowl with the mother of the groom." Pointing to an engagement picture on top of the pile she said, "That's the bride."

It was the first time she'd seen Hank with his jaw hanging open. "I can't believe you have the nerve to do this."

Just because he didn't have any big ambitions didn't mean no one else did. "Hank," she said, giving him a hurt look over her shoulder as she hurried out the door. "I'm doing it for Claire."

4

IT WAS THE FIRST TIME she'd seen him without a suit, and during the first few miles of their trip, Claire was wholly engrossed in her struggle not to ask Alec whether he felt naked without it. Theirs was a casual office, even by newspaper standards, and there was no dress code, per se, but Alec came to work each morning decked out in the uniform of corporate America. Claire suspected it was his way of showing he was at the top of the journalistic food chain.

The khakis and white polo he'd donned for this trip didn't subtract from the aura of power he wielded around the office. In fact, his casual clothes highlighted the fact that he had a body far more muscular than that of the stereotypical pencil jockey. She tried to ignore the sinewy muscles of his arm as he reached for the tape player, and the definition of his thigh as he braked and shifted gears. Claire resolved to stare at the scenery until they reached Loudon.

"How did you come to live in that house? Did you say it belonged to your grandparents?"

Damn. For months, the man had made it clear to her that she was no more worthy of his attention than a common housefly, and now, just when she needed for him to ignore her, he was trying to make small talk.

"Sort of," she said, her voice coming out as a croak. She cleared her throat and tried again. "They lived in a house on the same land, and they built that one for my parents when they first married. Years later, their own house started falling down around them, so they razed it and moved into the smaller one. After they died, my family could only justify keeping the land if someone wanted to live there.''

"So if not for you, your family would have made a killing with that property? Just asking."

She stared at him, exasperated. "I'm glad you aren't a real-estate agent. I can see you, calling me every morning at 8:00 a.m. sharp. 'Miss Morgan, have you changed your mind yet about selling?' 'Miss Morgan, I have it on good authority that your property taxes are about to sky-rocket'."

"I'm only trying to get to know you," Alec said. "Don't forget that I'm supposed to be your fiancé. I have to at least pretend I understand you."

So Alec thought he should try to understand her? He didn't know that *not* understanding her was what had made her so appealing to the guys who'd immediately started thinking about marriage at the first sight of her. They'd never looked beyond her girl you could take home to mama persona. But Claire knew that mama and her boy would probably faint if they ever caught a glimpse of the real inner her.

Sarcastic, a bit goofy, with thoughts that ran a hundred miles an hour. Scott was the only man with whom she'd shared that side of herself. When he'd rejected her, he'd rejected the real her. That was what made it so hard to accept.

Alec seemed oblivious to her growing moroser by the minute mood. "Listen, Claire. We've got less than an hour to synchronize our answers on this wedding thing. So start asking me some questions."

"Okay," she said. "When are we getting married?"

"December."

"No," she said automatically. "My parents married in December, and they spend their anniversary at the mall cafeteria while they Christmas shop. Let's say October. I can plan a wedding in five months. Is it small or large?"

"It's at your parents' house, and it's small."

"My parents retired to Florida last year," Claire said. "It's at your parents' house."

"My sister and her family live with my parents," he said. "It's so cramped, we couldn't even squeeze in a bridesmaid. So let's say it's going to be at one of those historic old homes around Ridgeville. We haven't decided which one yet, but we're leaning toward the Ramsey-Ivy house."

"That'll work," Claire said, admiring his taste. The Ramsey-Ivy house was one of her favorite local homes. She wondered if Alec really liked it, or if it was the first thing that popped into his head. "We're going to live in my house, right?"

"No," Alec said. "We're going to sell your house, take our share of the money and buy a condo."

"You have no soul," Claire told him. She tried to think of other questions people asked prospective couples. Dwelling on her own disastrous last engagement wasn't a good idea, so she tried to remember what she had asked women who told her they were engaged. "The ring," she said. "Where's my ring?"

"What ring?"

"The ring a man gives a woman when he asks her to marry him." She held up her left hand. "I don't have one."

"Not everyone has an engagement ring," Alec said. "Poor young couples like us can decide to get married, then scrimp and save for the ring."

Claire shook her head, surprised by how strongly she felt about this issue. She grabbed the tail of Alec's untucked knit shirt. "You spent at least seventy dollars on this shirt. You can afford to get me a ring."

"This was a seasonal markdown item last year, so it was just thirty-five dollars." He turned and stared at her. "Listen to yourself, Claire. You aren't serious, are you?"

"Yes, I am," she said, letting go of the shirt. "I'm not stepping out of the car at Miranda's unless I have a ring."

"Look," Alec said. "Be reasonable. We probably should have thought about this ring thing, but there's no way we're going to get one at this late stage."

"I'm sorry," she said stubbornly. "But we have to. I'm not going up there and facing Miranda and all her friends and family, just so they can all whisper about me when I leave the room. Isn't it a shame about Claire? Once again deluding herself into thinking she's getting married, when this jerk is too cheap to buy her a ring."

"I resent that," Alec told her. "Tell them I bought you one so big that you're afraid to actually wear it. Or tell them I bought you one but it's being sized."

Claire slouched in her seat. "Don't you think everyone will see through those lies?"

"Not if they don't see through the rest of the ones we're telling."

"That's my point," she said vehemently, so vehemently, in fact, that Alec swerved a little on the road before Claire grabbed the wheel. He pushed her hand away, the sudden contact leaving her even more rattled than she was before. She continued, trying to stay calm. "I think that the ring is the prop on which this whole charade is going to hinge."

Without warning, Alec pulled the car into a fast-food drive-thru restaurant and parked. "If this discussion is going to get any livelier, I'd like to be off the road for it. Claire, when a couple tells me they're engaged, I believe them. I don't question their relationship, and I don't start calculating in my head how much that rock set him back."

This had gone all wrong. She'd never meant to get so hysterical and materialistic. Over what? Over not getting a diamond from someone who probably wouldn't spare the fifty cents it would take to get a toy ring from a Cracker Jack box? She said quietly, "I think you look at everything with a cynical eye, and so do a lot more people than you expect. I think that if I were Miranda, and my old friend Claire showed up with someone that she was trying to pass off as a fiancé, but this Claire didn't have a ring, and the fiancé just happened to be a newspaper reporter—editor, I mean—I think I'd either put two and two together or pay someone to do it for me."

They sat in silence for a few moments, then Alec started the car. "I'm convinced," he said. His tone had lost its belligerence. "Since we're only a few miles out of town, we'll turn back and hit a pawnshop. Do you want to split the cost of it?"

Claire hesitated before speaking. "Actually, I know a way we could get a ring without either of us spending money." Cheered some, now that he seemed to be paying attention to her ideas, Claire began to outline her plan for Alec. "But first," she said, "let's swing through that drive-thru and get something to eat. All this arguing has left me starved."

DID HE DOUBT himself? Hank answered his own question. No, he did not doubt himself. It wasn't even noon yet, and he had already polished off all of his work. Even though no one else was in the office, force of habit made him download his articles onto a disk and shove it in his drawer. Everyone else uploaded their work straight into the paper's net server, where articles written by one writer were open to perusal by all. This meant that Alec, when feeling nitpicky, or Lissa, being bored, or Mick, trying to be helpful, would invariably scratch and poke at everyone else's stories until press time. He knew Claire did the same thing he did, handing Alec only hard copy and hiding the electronic copy somewhere untouchable until press time.

His own work behind him, Hank moved on to Lissa's rough draft, wondering where she was the day her journalism professor covered the difference between "draft" and "notes." A draft implied that sentences had been put together, paragraphs at least vaguely sketched out. This, instead, was a list of names, guests at the reception he supposed, with cryptic comments like "sixties sheath" and "chiffon ruffle thing" written out to the side.

"Where the hell is everybody?"

Hank looked at his watch. It was only eleven, a record for Mick. "Claire and Alec went to the taping, remember? You're here early."

"I've got to write a story. Kind of nervous about it," Mick said, hanging up his hat and pouring the remaining dregs of the coffee Hank had made earlier. "Where's Lissa?"

"She had to run an errand. I'm sure she'll be back," Hank said.

"I don't care one way or another," Mick told him. "If I didn't have this story breathing down my neck, I'd be out on my boat. You ought to head out early, too. When Alec's away, there's no better time to play."

With that, Mick disappeared into his office, and Hank, despite all his past confidence in Mick, couldn't help worrying a little about the mental sharpness of the man who seemed to forget that Alec worked for him, not the other way around. Hank was still brooding about how to stretch Lissa's scrawl into a story when the door to the publisher's office creaked open and Mick stuck his head out, paler than Hank had ever seen him before.

"Hypothetical question for you, buddy." Mick's voice rang out in false cheer. "Would it be possible for someone to throw the entire editorial content of the paper into the computer's trash?"

Hank's voice, when he could speak, was a whisper. "Did you empty it, too?"

Mick nodded.

ALL RIGHT, here was the new theory Alec was working on, one fueled, no doubt, by the greasy fast-food sausage and biscuit he'd just downed, followed by a twenty-ounce coffee to go. Claire had also graciously forked over some of her giant cinnamon roll, and the sugar high he was getting from that was probably contributing to his current line of illogical thought. Because he was on the verge of an idea so preposterous that he knew he wasn't thinking rationally. He was beginning to think Claire made him nervous.

He knew that all the evidence indicated that exactly the opposite was true. But what if her own nervousness was simply a reaction to his? What if he was the one who was jittery whenever he was around her, and she was so put off by his herky-jerky demeanor that it made her a wreck just to be near him? He thought back to the first time he'd met her, on the elevator headed upstairs. He had a clear vision of what she looked like that day. Her hair swung to the left side, and she had on an oversize white dress with pink flowers. He remembered feeling this odd jolt of recognition when he saw her, only it was the kind of feeling you get when you run into a college professor at the gym after you've faked a case of mono, or when you run into your landlord at an expensive restaurant when you haven't paid your rent in two months. He had this strange notion he'd disappointed her somehow.

Then she'd tripped him, and all that déjà-vu stuff was gone. Once he'd extracted his tie from between the elevator doors, he'd studiously avoided her, bounding out of the close space before the doors were barely open in his haste to get away from her. She'd followed him, and the rest was their history.

Revisionist history, he told himself. That's what he was engaging in, trying to talk himself into this crazy idea. Couldn't he point to plenty of times when he'd tormented Claire with his wicked coolness, while she'd quaked before him? Smiling to himself, he remembered some of them. There, he felt better. At least until he looked at Claire in the seat next to him, happily reading the daily paper without an apparent care in the world. She didn't even seem to mind that her dress had hiked up to an even more risqué level than its original one.

Alec tapped on the paper. "Trying to make friends with the truck drivers, Claire?"

She put the paper aside. "What?" She glanced down. "Oh, I understand." She yanked the fabric back down and primly crossed her legs at the ankles. Her mad blushing cheered him, and when he spoke again, he put a note of concern in his voice.

"Are you sure this is the right thing to do?"

"This whole trip is probably wrong-headed, and I think in my heart that I know that. But this at least gives me an excuse to do something I couldn't make myself do any other way," she said.

He had his own doubts about Claire's plan. To get a ring on her finger with minimal expense, she'd proposed using the engagement token she'd gotten from the notorious Scott. They were going to swing back by Claire's house to pick it up, then take it to a nearby pawnshop to trade for another one. He'd wondered why she couldn't just wear that one to the retreat, but the squawking and near-hysteria that ensued reminded him that Miranda had seen the ring. His next question was whether or not Claire was really fine with this. He stopped himself every time he started to ask, and they completed the trip back to her house in silence.

He left the engine running as she jumped out of the car and went back into the house. She returned less than a minute later, clutching the piece of jewelry in her palm. She buckled her seat belt, and they were off again.

"I'm surprised you didn't take the opportunity to pace the property off while you had the chance," Claire said.

Ignoring her wisecracks, he said, "Can I see it?"

She opened her hand, and he gazed at the glittery object sheltered there, not knowing what he was looking for. She closed her fist around it again. "I am, really," Claire said, "fine with this."

Startled, he glanced up at her. She went on. "Is that what you've been wondering?" When he nodded, she continued, "I think this is the perfect way to let go of this. I couldn't sell it, because I couldn't see being happy blowing the money on something frivolous. I'd think, this money I just spent once symbolized my whole future for me." Her voice dropped ominously. "What kind of future is that?"

He shivered involuntarily, then forced himself to get a grip. "So why didn't you throw it in the river? Women are always doing that in movies."

"No. That didn't seem satisfying, either. I'd have a moment of triumph. Then what? No, this way I actually get something tangible out of the deal." Although he'd seen Claire smile before, once or twice, those had been quiet smiles, half smiles. He had never seen this expression of warm optimism that she now wore, and he found that he liked it. "This can be a symbol of my new life as someone married to her job."

He had to lighten the mood a little. "As the paper's best and hardest-working life-style reporter."

He was braced for the whack on the chest he took from her rolled-up daily paper. "News, Alec," Claire said. "I'd hate to have to spill the truth to Miranda as soon as we get there. You know how sometimes I can't resist blurting out the first thing that comes to my mind."

"I've only recently noticed that particular trait." He cruised into the parking lot of Charlie's Pawnshop. "I once bought a watch here, and Charlie, the guy who runs it, is an okay guy. Unless there's someplace you'd rather go."

"No, this is fine," she said. "And to think that I believed the paper paid you enough to afford that elegant timepiece." Claire got out of the car and handed Alec the ring. "You do the talking."

Alec hadn't considered how suspicious it might sound to Charlie that they wanted to trade the ring for one of the same value, especially since they didn't have one already picked out. Charlie kept examining the diamond, checking it for flaws. Finding none, he asked Alec, "Why not just keep this one?"

It was a good question, and one that couldn't be answered truthfully. "Well," Alec said, "you see..."

Charlie interrupted him. "You got that watch here, didn't you?" Alec nodded. "How much did you pay for it?" When Alec reminded him of the figure, his expression lost some of its wariness. "That was a good deal from my side of the fence," he said.

"To use an apt expression," Claire said in a low voice. Alec kicked her in the ankle, and looked at the pawnbroker. Apparently a real sufferer of the same hearing ailment Alec had faked, he was oblivious to the bickering going on around him, once more checking the stone.

"You were going to tell me why you weren't keeping the ring?"

"Yes," Alec said, but before he could continue, Claire had pressed in front of him, leaning on the counter. Thinking she had forgotten exactly how low-cut her dress was, Alec took her shoulders in his hands, pulling her back next to him and putting his arm around her cozily. She pushed her hair behind her ear, a sure sign that he was making her nervous. He gave her shoulders a squeeze and waited to hear what she said next.

"My fiancé doesn't want to tell you why we're trading in this ring, because he's embarrassed." Before Alec could object, he felt her sharp elbow digging ever so slightly into his ribs. "See, this ring belonged to his great-aunt, whom he adored, and she wanted him to have it. Since he thought his aunt and uncle had a happy marriage, he took it from her. Well, once both of them had passed away, the true story came out. Her husband..."

"His great-uncle?"

"Yes. Her husband had been his own grandmother's first sweetheart, and he had bought this ring for his grandmother, until his great-aunt..."

"Her sister?"

"Yes, very good. Until her sister had spread terrible lies about her and taken her boyfriend away. Now, all the principals in this story have passed on, and so there's no reason why we shouldn't feel all right about using this ring, but it just seems kind of cursed, somehow. You know?"

Alec stared at Claire admiringly. Why had he ever thought she wouldn't make a good liar? She looked pretty pleased with herself, her cheeks flushed and her eyes sparkling. Then the man said, "And you think a ring that somebody traded in here is a better omen for your marriage?"

Claire's mouth tightened, and she stood up straight, shaking Alec's arm off of her. "Just give us a ring."

"All right, all right." He pointed to a glass case. "Anything on that second row, we'll call it an even trade."

Having expected Claire to grab a ring and go, Alec was annoyed to see her lingering over the various choices. "I'm not crazy about any of these," she said.

"You don't have to be crazy about any of them," he said. "It's not going to matter in the long run."

"That's not a very optimistic way to look at a new marriage," the owner said.

"What I meant was, we're in a bit of a hurry today. Pick one, Claire."

She had been bent near the glass case, examining the rings. Now she stood up with a dreamy look in her eyes. "You know what? I don't want a diamond. I agree with Anne of Green Gables, who waited all her life to see one, only to find it cold and ugly."

He'd already figured out that when Claire drifted into her childhood literary references, it spelled trouble for him. He tried to reason with her. "Engaged women wear diamonds, not something else."

She drifted to the next case and pointed to a ring there. "Look at this beautiful sapphire." Pressed, he would have admitted that it was indeed beautiful. A blue stone, marquise-cut, placed in a simple gold band. "I'm disillusioned by diamonds. I want this," Claire said.

"This is ridiculous. People will think I was too cheap to spring for the real thing."

"A little while ago, you didn't mind people thinking you were too cheap to spring for a ring at all." She pointed to it. "We'll take that one," she told Charlie.

"I might owe you five bucks or so," Charlie said, handing Claire the sapphire. When she slipped it on, it fit perfectly.

Alec started to say they'd call it an even trade, but Claire pointed to a manual Underwood typewriter on a nearby shelf. "Throw in that and it's a deal."

Charlie shrugged his approval, and Alec retrieved the machine. Used to the weight of his laptop, he buckled a little under the unexpected load, then glared at Claire as she giggled.

"What are you going to do with this?" he asked.

"Finish my Ridgeville story," she said. "I'll be in the car." She walked out of the building, leaving him trying to navigate the door while holding her behemoth of a type-writer. Charlie came out from behind the counter, and held the door open for him. As he started out, Charlie whispered, "A girl who's disillusioned with diamonds might be hard to handle."

He looked outside to see Claire leaning against the car, admiring her ring. "Don't worry," Alec told Charlie as he lumbered out the door. "I already figured that out."

"I DON'T KNOW HOW you did it, but it's gone." Patting Alec's computer, Sid from the software store turned to Mick and said, "When you throw something away, it stays thrown."

"Thanks," Mick said weakly, avoiding Hank's stern frown.

Hank couldn't believe what he was hearing. Just an hour earlier, Sid had told him this happened all the time, that bumbling editors, writers and other folks who shouldn't be let at computers without licenses were always throwing away important stuff: annual reports, client data bases, even whole hard drives. It was nothing, Sid said, that a halfway competent systems manager couldn't solve in fifteen minutes. Unfortunately, the paper didn't have a systems manager, competent or otherwise.

Having taken pity on Hank and Mick, Sid had scuttled over with his briefcase and his special retrieval software. As he'd poked around in the computer's gray matter, he'd said to Hank, "This is how those government guys get busted. They think they've destroyed the electronic paper trail, when really it's just lying there waiting."

Now, as he watched his new buddy Sid throw in the virtual towel, Hank grew anxious. "What about all those government secrets you told me about? Never really gone? Wasn't that what you said?"

"It was," he said. He gestured at Mick. "But they didn't have this guy working for them." Sid started packing up.

"I see," Hank said. "Thank you for your help." After he said goodbye to Sid, he sat down at Alec's desk and propped his feet up on it, thinking.

Mick spoke at last. "Good thing the paper's only been around a few years, isn't it? Otherwise, it would be something serious like 'first time in fifty years the *Trib* doesn't publish.' When you hear first time in four years, it doesn't sound so bad."

"We're putting out a paper." Hank surprised himself with his authoritative manner.

"We can't. We were cutting it close anyway, with all the editing Alec was going to have to do on Monday. But he and Claire have both filed lots of stories for this edition. They can't recreate them in an hour or two."

"I've got my stories. Maybe he kept copies of his somewhere." He doubted it, though. Alec never kept backups of anything he did, saying it was a waste of space in the computer's memory.

"If you're going to suggest getting him back here, don't bother," Mick said. "I told him not to leave the number where they could be reached." The red of embarrassment finally gave Mick back his color. "I was afraid if we had the number we'd call him about every little thing. He tried to give it to me, but I told him if something so bad he should know about it happened, I was sure he'd hear it on the TV news."

"So are you calling the local anchors, or shall I?"

"I'm going to get something to eat," Mick said. "Want to come?"

"You're not going anywhere," Hank said, trying to silence that nagging voice in his head that reminded him that he was talking to Mick Regan, the man whose journalistic exploits he had admired from afar, the man whose lectures he'd memorized word for word in j-school. It was this local hero, he told himself, who'd scrapped the writing that had been entrusted to their care. He hardened his heart.

"Have something delivered if you have to," Hank told him. "Until we're due at a barbecue cook-off at seven, we aren't going anywhere."

5

"I'M SUCH A MISERABLE idiot," Claire said, smacking herself on the forehead.

"Hey, now, you leave the insults to me," Alec said. "Is there anything in particular you've done wrong, or was this just a broad self-appraisal?"

Alec's car featured one of those modern cabin climate-control systems, and the temperature inside the car wasn't supposed to creep past sixty-eight. So why did Claire feel as though she were about to have a heatstroke? She lifted her hair off her neck, and started fanning herself with the paper.

"I forgot to tell them I'm a vegetarian. And I forgot to pack a bottle of wine in my suitcase like I was going to," Claire said.

Alec didn't look very worried. "What if you had to drink from the host's bar? Afraid Miranda Craig's going to slip something in your cocktail?"

Claire laughed, glad to have the upper hand for a moment or two. "You, my friend, are out of luck if you thought you were going to be imbibing high-quality beverages out here, because the Craigs don't drink."

"Old-fashioned?" Alec made the word sound like the first visible symptoms of a fatal disease.

"Old-fashioned."

Trying to steer with his knees, he dug into his pocket and pulled out a five, grabbing the wheel again just as Claire covered her eyes and screamed. She felt him put the bill in her lap.

"Five dollars," he said. "Says we get there to find this jaded crew of entertainment types swilling stuff a lot stronger than cheap wine. And don't worry about your peculiar eating habits. These people will have them, too. There'll be more pestos and pastas there than you could possibly scarf down."

Claire opened her eyes. "And what will you eat, if that's the case?" she asked him.

"There's going to also be a sizable minority of red-meat-eating, cigar-smoking he-men. I'm going to join their club."

She didn't doubt that. She could just see him flitting off somewhere to schmooze with Miranda's friends. Trying to make her request sound lighthearted, she said, "Don't abandon me to the clutches of that ruthless woman, okay?"

He reached down and encircled her wrist with his fingers. "I'll stick to you like handcuffs. I promise." His fingers, which she'd expected to be as cool as the rest of him, tingled where they touched her pulse, and she knew he could tell exactly how much he was suddenly making her heart race. Slowly, deliberately, she removed his hand.

"I don't think restraints are necessary," she tried to say lightly, but it came out as wispy and choked as anything she'd ever said to him.

"I don't know why you're so nervous," Alec said. "You, of all people, know that she puts her panty hose on one leg at a time."

"I know a lot more than that about her," Claire muttered.

"Like what?" Alec asked. "Something that wasn't in her book? She locked all her baby dolls in the closet or swindled some kid out of his ice-cream money?"

Claire couldn't understand why Alec thought Miranda was capable of nothing more malicious than petty elementary school high jinks. "What makes you think Miranda can do no wrong?"

"So she stole your fiancé." He shrugged. "That's old news."

"Gee, Alec, thanks for your concern." He glanced at her, as if wondering whether he'd really hurt her feelings, but she was too riled up to feel any stabs of pain over Scott and Miranda. "Okay, I've got something for you. You know the movie *All About Eve?*" She interrupted him as he started to speak. "And before you say Nancy Davis, it was Bette. Anyway, there's this scene where the scheming ingenue arranges for Bette to get stuck out of town so she can take her place in the play. Well, at the time, Miranda was in the play *Come Back to the Five and Dime, Jimmy Dean, Jimmy Dean.* She wanted a bigger part, one that had gone to Casey Lyle. Instead, she was Edna Louise, who goes to the bathroom real early in the play and doesn't come back for a while."

"This two seemingly unrelated plot snippets come together in a minute, don't they?" Alec asked. "I'm going to be real disappointed if they don't."

"Shut up," Claire said. "I talked Miranda into watching this movie with me one Saturday morning. Guess who just happens not to show up for the play that night? Casey Lyle."

"Miranda knocked her over the head and buried her alive somewhere, I guess?"

Claire ignored him. "Miranda paid this guy Casey had been dating to take her to the mountains and wait too long to hike back down, so that they had to stay overnight at a hiker's shelter."

Alec looked disgusted, although not, Claire guessed, at Miranda's actions. "I can't believe you expect me to buy this story. What difference does it make who plays who…"

"Whom," Claire corrected automatically.

"In some tiny play."

"That's the other part of the story," Claire said.

"I don't know if we've got room for another part. With James Dean and Bette Davis involved, the cast is getting pretty crowded as it is."

"Trent Daniels was in town, and she knew he was coming to the show. Now, I know that Trent Daniels is a joke now," Claire said, heading off Alec's protest, "but at the time he was one of the most promising young actors in Hollywood. He even got a little minipicture in the corner of the *People* cover one week. Before Miranda, he was the only actor from Ridgeville to ever make a dent in the business, and everybody was gaga over him. He brought a director friend of his who was casting an off-Broadway play. He gave Miranda her first big break."

She glared at him, daring him to contradict her story. Alec, smiling smugly, said, "I hate to hurt your feelings, Claire, but this Trent Daniels rumor is old news. He's always calling the paper to suggest Miranda did something devious to get access to his director friend, although he doesn't quite know what it was. He even says he slept with Miranda."

They were out in the country now, and Claire faked an interest in the hay bales and cows they passed before she turned to Alec and said, "They did."

"Watch your mouth," Alec told her.

She turned to him. "I picked her up at his hotel the next day." Guessing that his horrified expression meant that she was striking a nerve, Claire said, "I'm not saying she slept her way to the top. She was very good in that role. And she worked her butt off once she got to New York."

"What about the girl in the mountains?" Alec asked. "Why doesn't she say something?"

"She and Jason Butler fell in love that night. She switched from theater to nursing, and they got married.

They're grateful to Miranda, especially since she sends their kids Christmas presents every year.''

She knew she'd made at least a small crack in Alec's skepticism. "Why haven't you shared this story?"

"I've told you before that I'm not the kind of person who airs other people's business in public," Claire said. Then she realized that by telling Alec, that was exactly what she'd done. "And I don't want you to, either. I didn't tell you this so you could put it in your article."

He didn't answer, and soon they came upon the Craig estate, the wall around it visible well before they got to the driveway. It was an odd fortress on land so far out in the sticks that they hadn't passed a single car in the last five miles.

A Loudon county patrol car was parked in the grass next to the Craigs' gate. The officer stepped out and introduced himself as Jimmy, and told them he was acting as security for the weekend. He punched a code on a box next to the entrance, and the gate swung open.

Expensive trees and shrubs, both native and imported, beckoned all the way to the top of the long driveway. Once there, Alec whipped his car between a black Mercedes and a huge van, audiovisual equipment spilling from the van's open back door.

The house Miranda Craig had built for her parents may have been smack in the middle of east Tennessee, but that hadn't stopped the architect from going for a Spanish villa, stucco paradise look, rough cream brick with dark red tiles. The house meandered all over the bank of Fort Loudon Lake, the same lake that backed up to Claire's property. Her sense of geography was woefully off, she knew, and she didn't have any idea whether her house was just across the lake or miles down the road from the opposite shore. But more than anything, she was flooded with a desire to be home.

"I don't want to do this," she started to tell Alec, but he sat with the keys in the ignition, making no move to get out of the car.

"She knew the part already," Alec said.

"She'd hoped that the director would change his mind, but he was really mad at Miranda at the time. She'd also been hoping something would happen to Casey. I just don't think she'd thought of speeding it along."

"Who played Miranda's part?"

She smiled at him. "Guess."

He nodded, as if he suspected as much already. "You knew the role from running lines with her, I guess." She barely had time to wonder at his sympathetic smile before he said, "Poor kid. Good thing you spent most of your time offstage."

Claire had only a few seconds to wonder if that was meant to sound as insulting as it did before Alec jumped out of the car and came around to her side. "Be sweet, Claire," he whispered.

"Remember," she whispered back, "what I told you is not for the record."

Not bothering to respond, he hauled her out of the car, and she got her bearings just long enough to hear her name shouted in a girlish Southern shriek.

"Claire. Oh my goodness, it's really Claire." The tanned, blond woman hurled herself at Claire. "Oh, I knew you'd come."

Claire stepped back from her oldest friend, who was now sniffling back tears, and was surprised to find that her own throat had tightened a little. She heard herself say, "Hey, Missy. How are you?"

"Wait, stop." A beefy arm interjected itself between them. From her irregular reading of *People* magazine, Claire recognized the man as Larry Cole, Miranda's personal manager. "Sweetie, sugar, it's . . ."

"Miranda, I know," Claire said. "It just slipped my mind for a second. It won't happen again."

Miranda stamped her expensively shod foot on the ground. "Larry. This is not for tape. I don't know why you have to barge in on everything you think is your business."

"Making this weekend run smoothly is my business," he said.

Miranda's fit of sweet sentimentality had passed, and she was all business now. "But maybe Claire should call me Missy?" Miranda asked. "That's how she knows me, after all."

Claire backed away from Miranda, annoyed with herself for the split second she'd allowed herself to miss her old friend. No matter what her former pal said, it was clear to Claire that publicity and attention were still Miranda's main concerns, and that trying to repair their friendship was not at the top of the list.

"Yes, don't forget that I've been a country bumpkin these past few years, and was completely unaware that my friend Missy had changed her name and become a Hollywood legend," Claire interrupted, but they didn't seem to hear her.

"It'll confuse the audience," Larry said stubbornly.

"Ask Christine's people about it," Miranda countered.

Claire felt Alec's mouth near her ear. "Do you think both of them played guitar in rock bands in college?"

She turned her face toward his, and said in a low voice, "Maybe Miranda should donate the proceeds of her next movie to research into the problem of selective hearing."

While they were whispering, an assistant of Larry's was dispatched to ask an assistant of Christine Colby's whether Claire should say "Missy" or "Miranda." Alec was just removing his lips from the vicinity of Claire's hair when Miranda's attention fell on them again. She put her hand over her mouth.

"I forgot to ask you all about this guy you're snuggling up to. Who could he be?" Miranda reached her hand out for Alec's, but Claire was suddenly determined that Miranda wouldn't touch him as long as she could help it. She preempted the move by taking both of his hands in hers and gazing into his eyes. "This is Alec Mason, my fiancé. He edits the newspaper where I work."

Miranda's tone was coy.

"And do you have a ring?"

Claire covered Alec's foot with her sandaled one, putting just a fraction of her weight on it to get the point across. She pulled her hand away from his, and showed Miranda the ring.

"An amethyst...."

"Sapphire," Claire interrupted. Hadn't Miranda played a geologist in a movie once?

"Of course. I get all the lesser stones mixed up. It's beautiful."

"Thank you," Claire said. She put her arm around Alec's waist and pulled him close to her, shocked at her own boldness, certainly, but shocked also by the way she could feel his heart racing near hers. "His great-grandfather spent his life savings on the stone so he could bring it with him from Scotland when he came to America to find his childhood sweetheart. He gave it to her, and it's been in the family ever since. We just had it put in a new setting."

Although Claire was personally touched by her invented story, Miranda's attention had already wandered. "How sweet," Miranda said. "Come and see everybody." She hooked her arm around Claire's waist, and pulled her along with her. Claire had no choice but to drop her hold on Alec and go. Propelled by Miranda, she reached out behind her to gesture to Alec to follow.

"Everybody, Claire's here with her fiancé." A chorus of greetings rose up from beside the pool, although Claire only recognized a couple of the faces. Miranda turned to her parents, who were dragging chairs out to the poolside. "Look, Mama. Isn't Claire pretty?"

Claire thought she heard an element of surprise in that question, but she forgot all about it, enveloped in a hug from Miranda's mother and a hearty handshake from her father. But when the elder Craigs disappeared to help the sound men find electrical outlets, Miranda repeated, "I've got to tell you, Claire. I didn't expect you to look so fabulous." Claire noticed her annoyed glance at Chris, her cousin, sunning himself on a deck chair.

"Reports of my recent frumpiness have been greatly exaggerated," Claire said cheerfully.

"I can see that now," Miranda said, watching as Chris waved weakly to Claire and threw a towel over his face. "I guess that's what happens when you get your information from unreliable sources." With one last lingering glare at Chris, Miranda changed the subject. "Listen, I want you to meet some of the other people who are here," she said. "There are hors d'oeuvres by the pool, so feel free to indulge." She stepped a few paces ahead of Claire, stepping up to the table laden with food. "I, of course, have to starve myself in the interest of my career, but you don't have to worry about that. No one expects a reporter to be svelte."

"No, but I bet they expect their actresses to have chests," Claire heard herself mutter softly. She knew Miranda couldn't hear her, but she hadn't realized that Alec could until she heard him gasp and choke beside her. Unlike many other people, who thought of the perfect comeback hours after the moment had passed, Claire had always shot back with instant retorts in her head. But until this recent crisis with Alec forced her to fall back on her verbal skills, she had never vocalized any of her smart-mouthed comments. Now she couldn't stop.

Miranda turned back to her. "Did you say something?"

Alec answered for her, putting his arm around her again as he did so. "She was telling me everything was so scrumptious, she was going to find it hard to resist the temptation."

Some kinds of temptation were easier to resist than others, Claire thought to herself as she felt Alec's arm circling her waist. Stuffed mushrooms and chocolate-covered strawberries were nothing compared to the feel of Alec's hand on her. Although there was no way she could slip out of Alec's grasp, she forced herself to ignore him as they listened to Miranda's introductions to the people around the pool. Claire was ordinarily good with names and faces, but the phalanx of hairdressers, makeup artists, seamstresses, junior publicists and production assistants blended into one indistinguishable lump. The only person who stood out of that crowd was Renee, Miranda's tall and intimidating psychic. All of them, as Alec had predicted, were munching on pestos, salsas and other vegetarian fare. Miranda's personal manager, Larry, who was downing shrimp and gourmet meatballs, had joined some of Miranda's aunts, uncles and cousins in the meat-eating contingent, although the women, at least, were not yet smoking cigars.

A door at the back of the house opened, and Claire recognized the woman who walked out—Christine Colby. Miranda waved her over. "Christine, this is my old friend Claire."

"Thank goodness you're here." Christine Colby walked up to Claire and Alec and shook hands with both of them. "Finally, the friend. Someone who isn't related to Miranda."

The friend? As in Miranda's only one? If that were true, then Miranda had no friends at all. Claire told herself the wealth and privilege accorded Miranda more than made up for her lack of companions, especially if she treated them all as callously as she'd treated Claire. Still, Claire caught herself feeling a bit sorry for her.

Fortunately the feeling passed. Miranda said, "I have other friends, of course, some of the people in my movies, but they're all tied up in L.A. and New York. An actor I've been seeing may fly out here tonight, but everyone else has been filmed at their home base. Christine is going to fit their comments into the show in such a way that it won't exactly be obvious that they weren't here. That way, they can be part of this without having to fly out to the middle of nowhere."

"Isn't that nice," Alec interrupted, giving Claire a hard squeeze. She assumed it was meant to be a warning of sorts. If so, she ignored it.

Claire smiled at Miranda. "But I can't imagine why any of your friends would want to miss the chance to meet the little people who made you who you are." She indicated the buffet table at the pool, where Miranda's loud aunt Fay was embroiled in a tussle over the last piece of shrimp with one of Miranda's more heavily tattooed cousins. "The only ones missing from this event are Scott Granville and our drama teacher, Mrs. Schibley."

Forcing Scott's name from her lips took something out of her, and when Christine Colby said, "Actually," Claire's heart fell to the floor, thinking she was about to say Scott was there. What would she say? How would she react? Would she want to slap him or run into his arms? Instead, Christine pointed to a far corner of the lawn. There, the cursed Mrs. Schibley was sternly lecturing a man Claire recognized as one of Hollywood's leading voice coaches, the one Miranda hired every time she needed to transform her native twang into something else.

"Mrs. Schibley," Claire said. "How nice."

"Don't you want to run down and say hi?" Miranda asked.

"That's okay," Claire said, pretending to take the idea seriously. "I'll catch up with her later."

"Let me show you your room," Miranda said. Claire wondered why she wasn't also showing Alec his, but didn't mention it as they tagged along behind Miranda. Christine said she'd brief Claire later, whatever that meant, and went off in search of other nostalgic prey. They entered the house through the back door near the pool, and Miranda said, "Mama will want to give you the whole tour later, but I'm sure you're too exhausted now to take it all in. You'll find an itinerary in your room, but for right now, why don't you all take a nap, watch movies or whatever, then join us in the casual dining room for dinner at six?" They walked through a sumptuously carpeted hallway, some of the doors down the hall open to identically laid-out spacious bedrooms. Miranda stopped in front of an open door and paused, leaning on the door frame. "No matter how hard I try, I can't convince my family that civilized people don't eat before eight. Also, you're in one of the drinking rooms, meaning there's a minibar stashed in the cabinet. That's mine and Mama's compromise, because she didn't want to have any drinks. I mean, she's become more open-minded, but her and Daddy's families are the same as ever. If you want cocktails, fix them yourself before dinner. That's what everyone else in the drinking rooms is going to do."

"And when everyone shows up soused, aren't your relatives going to think something funny is going on?" Claire asked.

"Oh, well, don't worry about that," Miranda said. "It'll mostly be the personnel I've brought with me, and everyone expects show business people to act funny anyway. You and Chris are the only ones who'll seem odd, and you're both a little eccentric." She waited a beat before she added, with a disarming smile, "I mean in a good way."

"And Alec? Is he in a drinking room, as well? Just so Chris and I won't be alone in our touched states?"

Miranda raised an eyebrow, and her lip curled up in a half smile. Claire recognized it as her "skeptically amused" look, one she had perfected in an English drawing room comedy they'd done in high school.

"You two are sharing a room, of course," she said.

"What did you say?" They spoke in one voice.

Miranda put her hand to her throat. "My goodness. For two people who plan to spend their lives together, you two act awfully horrified at the idea of sleeping in the same room." She put her hands on her hips and said, in an exaggerated accent that had a lot more to do with Dixie than it did with Appalachia, "Are y'all sure you're engaged?"

Alec laughed, an odd, forced chuckle that cascaded through the large hall. Miranda joined him, and the two of them continued their "ha-ha's" and "hee-hee's" as Claire glanced at her watch, waiting for their fit of jolliness to pass.

"What a funny question," Alec said. He reached for Claire and crushed her in an enthusiastic bear hug. Her neck was twisted, and she was caught off balance, Alec being the only thing that held her up, but she had to admit to herself that the experience was, on the whole, far from terrible. She could feel once again the comforting beat of Alec's heart, and she could smell his clean, expensive-smelling soap and his well-laundered shirt. "It's just that Claire told me your parents were old-fashioned, and so we had steeled ourselves for a night of sneaking into each other's rooms. I'm so glad that we don't have to." He tilted Claire's head toward him. "Aren't you, honey?"

"Quite," she said, the word coming out in a raspy whisper as Alec held her in his solid grip.

Although Claire thought, privately, that anyone with a shred of acting talent wouldn't have been fooled by Alec's performance, Miranda seemed satisfied. "Enjoy yourselves," she said. "Let me know if you need someone to help you with your bags."

"Thanks," Alec said, practically dragging Claire into the room with him. He stuck his head back out the door. "Very pleased to meet you, Miranda."

Claire heard a faint "You too, Alec" before she decided she'd had all the toadying up to Miranda she was willing to tolerate for the day. As she grabbed the belt loops of Alec's khakis and pulled him back into the room with her, she heard the outside door close at the far end of the hallway. Alec closed their own door behind him, and they were alone together. As one, the two of them turned to stare at the queen-size bed in the middle of the room. Then they turned to look at each other. When Claire saw Alec step an almost imperceptible half inch forward, she moved as well. They looked at each other again, then both of them bolted for it, landing in a tangle on top of the spread. Their voices rose together with the cry, "I was here first."

NO ETIQUETTE EXPERT or fashion maven had covered the do's and don'ts of crashing a weekend get-together, so Lissa had to improvise her own guidelines. Scott expected the two of them to be tossed out of Miranda's within seconds, and she had to admit it was likely. But if for some reason she and Scott—or just her, for that matter—were welcomed into the bosom of the party, she didn't want to be stuck wearing the same outfit for the rest of the weekend. On the other hand, she mused as she flipped through her closet, it would certainly look presumptuous if she showed up with a well-stocked suitcase full of flashy and glamorous outfits. She compromised, putting together a small collection of pants and tops in complementing colors, along with a variety of accessories. She wanted people to notice how good she looked, while still finding it plausible that she was cleverly rearranging the same set of clothes.

It was Lissa's experience that planes never arrived until at least fifteen minutes after their announced time, so she got to the airport about twenty minutes past the hour she and Scott had agreed upon. After leaving her car with its flashers on in the passenger loading zone, she made her way to the appropriate gate, expecting to see a lone and tormented bachelor wondering if she'd abandoned him. Instead, she came across a gang of cranky and tired friends and family, all of them waiting for passengers on Scott's plane.

She found an abandoned issue of *Glamour,* one she'd skimmed several months earlier. She tried to read it, forcing herself to ignore snoring senior citizens as well as a toddler who was launching kick after kick at the cola machine. When a cheer from the crowd announced the arrival of the plane, she watched, impatiently, as businessmen strode past quickly, and as chattering college kids got off the plane in pairs and groups. One devastatingly handsome man, one of the few solo males not dressed in a suit, got off by himself, looked around for a moment, then walked away. Whoever was supposed to pick him up is missing a golden opportunity, Lissa thought as she watched him disappear. She turned her attention back to the crowd disembarking from the plane, but she didn't see anyone who resembled Scott. Had he chickened out on her?

Obviously, he had. As the crowds ebbed away, leaving her in the middle of their empty candy wrappers and discarded cola cans, she saw that Mr. Handsome had returned. He glanced around, his eyes passing over Lissa, then returning to her.

"Who stood you up?" he asked. His smile told her what he thought of that person.

She flashed her own set of teeth back at him. "Nobody really. My friend's geeky ex. What about you?"

"I was going to help some girl reporter out, but I guess she got a bigger story."

The realization of what they'd each said hit her. "Scott?"

"Lissa?"

"But I've seen a picture of you," Lissa sputtered. "You weren't at all handsome."

"That picture in Miranda's book?" he asked her. "She chose that one specifically because it made me look like a dork." As they walked to the baggage claim area, he said, "I hope you're as pleasantly surprised as I am. I had no idea you'd be so pretty."

She blushed at this bit of flattery, then stopped herself from returning a bit of her own. He was too cute to flirt with casually, and if he was going to persist in charming her this way, they might never get to Loudon. Besides, she reminded herself guiltily, there was Claire. "Scott," she said, giving him what she hoped was just a friendly smile. "Where we're going, you've got two angry ex-girlfriends waiting for you. Don't make your life any more complicated."

Was it her imagination or was his own smile just a little tinged with regret? He picked up a duffel bag at the claim area, and she followed him out the door.

"Where's your car?" he asked.

"Right there," she said, pointing. Pointing, she realized, at empty space. "It was right there. My car's been stolen." She flagged down a nearby security guard. "My car. It was right there. My car's been stolen."

"Been towed," he said. "This is a restricted area. Can't leave your car there all day."

"It is a zone for loading and unloading of passengers. It's not my fault if his airline was so irresponsibly late."

She turned to Scott, and allowing just the tiniest note of heartbreak to slip into her voice, asked him, "What'll we do now?"

He put his duffel bag on the sidewalk and sat down on it before saying, "Lissa, honey, I don't have a clue."

6

SHE WAS GOING TO HAVE to get rid of that distracting dress, Alec concluded. Put on something befitting a responsible and serious adult, and shed the provocative, playful look she'd tried out today. He would tell her it didn't suit her. Just as soon as he could make himself stop staring at her.

Claire scrambled to a sitting position on the bed and scooted away from him on the bed. "What are you staring at?"

You, he wanted to say, but he didn't.

She flipped her hair back over her shoulders with her typical self-conscious gesture, then moved from the bed to the room's sofa. "You can have the bed," she said. "I don't sleep anyway."

Seeing her there, so distant from him, he became unaccountably irritated. He knew it was unreasonable, but the experience of Claire walking away from him made him feel like a bridegroom whose newly beloved had locked herself in the bathroom for the night. He sat up on the bed, and when he spoke, his voice was harsh.

"You know, statistics show that most of the people who claim to be total insomniacs are actually getting plenty of rest every night. They just like to complain about how tired they are. I bet you'll sleep plenty tonight."

He remembered the good old days of a few days ago, when his diatribes left her all aflutter. It was an endearing trait, he thought. Now she looked at him with amusement. "Alec," she said, "we are not in a competition to see who can down the most sleeping pills in one night's stay. I only meant that where I sleep isn't that big a deal to me, so feel free to take the bed. I was just trying to annoy you when I said I wanted it earlier, but now I see I've annoyed you even more by not wanting it." She shrugged, as if to say, What's a sensible girl like me to do, locked in the room with a maniac like this?

The bed no longer held its appeal for him, since he wasn't fighting Claire for it. He got up and looked around the room, flicking the light on in the roomy bathroom, opening the empty dresser drawers. He slid the closet doors open and was greeted by a stack of fresh bed linens and a row of empty hangers. "This is the first guest room I've ever stayed in where the hosts weren't using the closets and dressers to store junk."

"I guess if you had a jillion guest rooms, you'd probably run out of junk on the first few," Claire said.

"No. I wouldn't have any junk to store. You, though, would probably stick something in all jillion."

She sat up on the couch. "You saw my house. It was clean."

"Clean, yeah, but I can tell you're a pack rat."

"And you aren't?"

"If I don't need it, I toss it out."

"Very cold-blooded of you," Claire said.

Alec poked around some more, coming across the refrigerator and minibar in the corner of the room. "I guess I win the five dollars," he said.

"Certainly not. In order for you to win the five dollars, we would have had to see all those people out in the open, drinking. If they're doing it behind closed doors, then all bets are off."

"I can't believe these people," he said. "They object to seeing an open bottle of wine outside, but they'll let people fornicate in their rooms all they want."

Claire put her hands over her ears. "I hate that word."

"Fornicate?"

"I'm warning you. Don't say it again." She shuddered.

Alec sighed and plopped himself down on the couch beside her. "This is a hell of a mess. I'm sharing a bedroom with a girl who blushes at the word *fornication*. And, you know, you haven't been as friendly to Miranda as you could be."

She tucked her legs under her and slid away from him a bit. "You're wrong," she said. "I've definitely been as friendly as I can be."

"But can't you pretend that you're trying to get right back to being best friends with her? At least for my sake?"

"She's not going to blame you for my behavior," Claire said. "In fact, you could probably go up there right now and pour your heart out to her, telling her how difficult and unreasonable I am. Ask her if, as my oldest friend, she has any pearls of wisdom for you."

"That's not a bad idea," he said. He was beginning to have a budding admiration for Claire's talent for deception. Too late, he saw that he had misread her.

"Don't you dare," she said. Her eyes were angry, and her cheeks were flushed. She wasn't teasing.

"Claire, calm down." He took her hand and gave it what he hoped was a reassuring squeeze. "I was only kidding. You know I would never betray you." Having taken her hand, he didn't want to let it go. He held on to it firmly, hoping she wouldn't pull it away.

She didn't. "Anyway, I'd say that Miranda feels better with me not embracing her with open arms. I think it makes her feel like she's paying her dues."

He opened his mouth to disagree with her, but felt her soft hand in his and reconsidered.

"All in all," Claire continued, "I think it's going pretty well. This lying stuff isn't as difficult as I believed it would be."

That was an understatement. Claire was so good at it, in fact, that he wasn't sure she hadn't been a con artist in another life. No need, though, to let her get too overconfident. "You spun some elaborate tales, all right. You had my family trading gemstones back and forth so fast that I was considering opening up my own jewelry store."

She looked at their two hands joined together and said, "Aren't there some pearls or opals stashed at the family manse somewhere?"

"The closest thing we have to a family manse is the mining camp where my great-grandparents lived before they moved to town. My great-grandfather might have brought my great-grandmother a lump of coal and a celebratory bottle of moonshine, but that's about it for the finer things in life."

He wished he could read the look she gave him. "I thought you were some snotty-nosed rich kid, someone who took privilege for granted."

He didn't tell her that he had spent most of his life cultivating that air. By some fluke of public school zoning, he'd gone to school with rich kids, and had just naturally fit in with them, adapting their habits, acquiring their tastes. He'd never deliberately tried to pass himself off as someone with money, but he hadn't tried to correct that impression, either.

Claire continued. "So if you aren't from some swanky family, then why are you so hard-hearted about my land? Where's your populist edge?"

"I don't have one of those," he said. "I believe in progress. Let that area develop the way it's going, rather than sitting on your property yelling about being poor but proud."

Playing devil's advocate came so naturally to him that he had opened his mouth and challenged her to an argument without even thinking about the immediate consequences. It was at that moment she seemed to realize there was something very strange about two people who were always at odds with each other sitting cozily on a couch holding hands. In an instant, she had jerked her hand away from him.

Rather than call attention to her action, Alec continued the debate by himself, trying to draw Claire in. "You didn't stay here your whole life. You moved away... went to graduate school, if I remember correctly. What's that if not trying to make a little progress with your life?"

She laughed. "Oh, that. Believe me, graduate school had nothing to do with progress. I wanted to go somewhere where I could get paid to read while I decided what I wanted to do with my life. After a while, I figured out I didn't ever want to be a teacher, and I couldn't see any other career use for an encyclopedic knowledge of the Victorian poets. That's when I started free-lancing for the local papers. I realized I was good at it, and I decided I wanted to follow that career when I moved back to Ridgeville."

It had never occurred to him to ask why Claire had moved back to town. He had never been interested before. "Is the house the only reason you moved back? So your family wouldn't sell it?"

She shrugged. "That, and besides, if you've seen one college town, you've seen them all. There's always one good bookstore, one good health food store, one arty movie house. I thought, I might as well be home."

He had this strange need to keep her talking, maybe because of all the times he'd ignored her or treated her rudely. It was almost as though this room were a sort of magical place, one that let the real Claire shine through in such a way that he could see and appreciate her. "Victorian poets?" Alec reached way back into the recesses of his brain for information from sophomore English class. "Robert Barrett?" he ventured.

Her smile was real and warm, and if it was a bit at his expense, that was all right. "Robert *Browning*," she said. "You were close. Actually, my master's thesis was going to be on Ernest Dowson." At his raised eyebrows and shrug, she said, "You might not know the name, but you know the poem." Leaning back on the couch, one leg crossed over the other and her hands clasped over her knee, she began to recite. "Last night, between her lips and mine there fell a shadow . . . and I was desolate and sick of an old passion. I have been faithful to thee, Cynara! in my fashion."

Alec knew a few things about himself. He was cynical, and he was practical. He had never wept over a television show or a book, and he hadn't cried at the movies since his aunt took him to see *Old Yeller*. Even the telephone company commercials that got everybody else left Alec cold. So how was it that this sentimental poem, written by a guy who'd been dead for a hundred years, could bring a lump to his throat?

Claire. Seeing her, so close to him, he was suddenly grateful that they weren't holding hands any longer. If they had been, then it would have been the most natural thing in the world for him to kiss her. Only later would they have remembered that the two of them being together was the most unnatural thing in the world. Wooed by the luxury around him, the congenial atmosphere, Alec was letting himself slip into a daze. He'd almost forgotten that he'd come here to work, not to get all mushy and dewy-eyed over a woman who was his polar opposite.

"I've got to go," he said, jumping up. "Lovely poem, really."

She stared at him with wide eyes. "Alec," she said. "We aren't expected at dinner till six."

"I know. That only leaves me a few hours to track down Miranda and start to work on this right away. First, I have to soften her up about the paper. Then the real work starts." He rummaged through the desk drawer, looking for a pen, and came up with one on the first try. Paper, however, was another story. The only type he could find in the desk was heavy, scratchy and expensive—suitable for writing thank-you notes to sorority sisters and starlets, but nothing any self-respecting reporter would carry around. He turned to Claire. "You don't have a notebook I could borrow, do you?"

She opened her purse and took out a fresh one. "Good luck. And remember, don't ask her about what I said."

If she was sorry to see him go, she didn't say so. Probably she was as eager as he was to nip this hand-holding and secret-whispering in the bud and get their relationship back on its usual troubled and bumpy track. Thinking, though, that he ought to say something more to her than a casual "See you later," he thought for a second, then said, "You know, sometimes I like to argue for the sake of arguing. I don't really have a lot of feelings on a subject one way or the other. You know that, don't you?"

She grinned. "I do now."

With the distinct feeling that he had just given solace and comfort to the enemy, Alec headed out in search of Miranda.

A TIME WARP or a parallel universe? Claire wished she were up on her science-fiction terminology. Which could better explain the phenomenon that had just happened in this room? She and Alec, holding hands. She and Alec speaking to each other as reasonable adults.

She looked down at the dress, then cringed a little, thinking of all times that day she'd forgotten how low-cut it was. Surely that wasn't the sole reason for Alec's change in attitude about her? Probably not. After all, he was so handsome that he didn't have to wait around for ugly ducklings. He always had his choice of swans.

Like Miranda? No way, she thought to herself. Alec may be handsome, but Miranda was way out of his reach. Everyone knew that glamorous Hollywood types sought out other glamorous Hollywood types. But, argued a nagging voice, what about all those starlets who are married to lawyers and restaurant magnates and CEOs? You see them in the magazines. Restaurant magnates, maybe, she thought, but not the editor of a middling weekly paper. With his skills though, the impudent voice continued, she could swing him some cushy job as a screenwriter's consultant. But why would she want him? Claire asked herself again. The answer came immediately. Because you do.

Maybe getting down to work would shut off all these niggling thoughts in her head. Occupy her subconscious, make it work for her and not against her. Claire slipped out of her room, and headed for a stairwell opposite the end of the hall that led out to the pool. There had to be a way for her to get out without having to go through the torture of watching Alec fall at Miranda's feet.

But why was it torture? Let's face it—by bringing him along and labeling him her fiancé, she might as well be hanging a sign over his head saying Fresh Bait! Hadn't she told Lissa that if she had real feelings for Alec, she'd be happy to bring him along with her, just to show how deeply she trusted him? How had Lissa ever listened to that lie with a straight face? If Claire had any real feelings for Alec, she'd be ready to shove him in the car and hightail it back to Ridgeville. Which was exactly what she wanted to do.

She crept up the steps and found herself in a large foyer. A sunny, Southwestern weaving hung from one wall, and a rough butcher's block held a green glass jar full of flowers. Mrs. Craig had always liked the rustic look, and Claire was glad to see that her home still reflected her tastes, even if the house did cost about ten times as much as her last one. Hoping against hope that she wouldn't set off some kind of security alarm, Claire opened the front door and crept out toward Alec's car.

Even though she had him pegged as the type who kept his doors locked everywhere he went, she was pleasantly surprised to discover that the car was open. Bad manners, she suspected, to lock up your possessions at a house full of rich people and guarded by a security man. While she was trying to decide between the typewriter and one of her suitcases, she heard a car pull up and saw it park two spots away from Alec's. She had finally decided to try carrying both, and was lifting the typewriter out of the trunk when she heard a voice shout, "Wait. Let me give you a hand."

The voice sounded familiar. She turned, nearly losing the typewriter in the process, and feasted her eyes on Josh, the redeeming spot in an otherwise terrible movie about teenagers and the teachers who try to civilize them. "You're Josh," she said. "From *Looking In On the Outside.*"

He swung the satchel he carried onto his back, then took the typewriter from her hands. He said, "I can't believe you saw that movie. It grossed around fifty dollars."

She leaned against the open trunk. "I review movies for a living, so unfortunately I can't claim to have been a paying customer."

"Fortunately," he told her.

"You don't have to feel embarrassed about your performance. You really stood out in that movie." She started to close the trunk but he stopped her.

"Do you want some help carrying in the rest of this stuff?" he asked, peering in at the other suitcases.

"Oh, no, that's okay, really. Alec will get it."

"Who's Alec?"

"He's my ed . . . um, my fiancé."

He grinned at her. "Are you sure?"

"Fairly sure," she said. "I'm sorry, I can't remember your real name."

"Roger Walker. And you're?"

"Claire Morgan."

"Oh, Miranda's friend."

Claire wondered if Christine and company had made some sort of announcement to that effect. Step right up and see Miranda's chump of a friend. She pointed in the direction of the pool, still clogged up with poor relations. "A lot of people are there, if you want to socialize. I don't see Miranda anywhere."

"Oh, I do," he said. He pointed beyond the pool, down to the rolling pasture and the man-made pond. Claire squinted mightily, but without her glasses, she couldn't see anything more than a group of random little blurs, walking around as if in one mass.

"Where's your fiancé?" he asked.

"I don't know. He went to find Miranda, to talk to her about doing an interview for the paper we work for. But if he isn't out there with her, I don't know where he is."

Roger looked toward the field again. "There's a guy with brown hair and a white shirt trailing around after the group, bouncing from here and there to try to get closer to Miranda."

"That's him," Claire said.

Roger smiled at her. She saw that although playing a teenager had been a bit of a stretch for him, he was still a good couple of years younger than she was. "Are you going to the pool?" he asked.

"I don't think so. I think I'm just going to go rest until dinner," she said.

She walked around to the front door, with Roger following her. "I guess I should check in with Mrs. Craig and find out where I'm staying," he said.

"Do you know the Craigs?" she asked.

"I met them once a few months ago," he said. "Miranda had them flown to Hollywood to celebrate their wedding anniversary, and I tagged along."

It clicked in Claire's mind then. This was the actor Miranda had been seeing, the one who was going to try to fly down to join them. She didn't mean to be so blunt, but she blurted it out anyway. "So you're Miranda's boyfriend, then?"

He blushed, his neck turning red first, then his cheeks. "I wouldn't say that. The papers write it that way sometimes, but then the next week they'll print a picture of her partying the night away with a real actor."

He seemed so sweet. What a shame he had to have fallen into Miranda's clutches. But at least his being here would keep her away from Alec, that little voice chimed.

She tried to make him feel better. "You're a real actor. You're going to be in some great movies someday."

Roger blushed again. "Well, thanks."

"No, really," Claire continued. "Someday Miranda will be the one the press barely notices, and you'll be the one photographed with all of the hottest young starlets." Realizing after the fact that he might be offended at any criticism of Miranda, she backtracked. "I mean, not that your success has to come from Miranda's failure. There's room at the top for both of you, I'm sure."

"I understand," he said, smiling. His brown eyes crinkled at the edges, and a sudden breeze whipped his longish blond hair.

"I'd better get back to my room," she said, "And let you find yours." She opened the door and walked back downstairs, Roger following her with the typewriter. At her room, she peeked in to see if Alec was there. Of course not. She wondered if he'd had any luck catching up to the elusive and flighty Miranda, and hoped, perversely, that he hadn't.

Claire set her suitcase down by the door and took the typewriter from Roger. "Listen, it was very nice meeting you."

"It was nice meeting you, too, Claire. It's been a long time since I've run into anybody who thought I was an okay actor. That made me feel good." He smiled in such a deliberately charming way that she knew that smile must be his trademark, his ticket to becoming a future heart-throb. "I hope I see you later."

"I hope so, too," she said.

"And your fiancé," he said.

"Oh, of course," Claire said. "I can't wait for you to meet Alec." They said goodbye, and she heard him lope up the stairs. After she closed the door, Claire laid her suitcase on the bed and took out the demure floral dress she'd planned to wear to dinner. Shaking it out in front of her, her eye was caught by the dress that was packed beneath it in the suitcase. This was the red number Allie had convinced her to buy and forced her to pack, the dress Claire had sworn would go straight to some charity group before it ever appeared on her body. It was the last one on the rack, a perfect fit, and on sale—all factors that made Allie claim Claire was fated to own this dress. She'd argued and protested, but now she was coming around. Not only was she meant to own this dress, she decided, she was meant to wear it tonight.

She was reapplying her makeup in the bathroom when Alec stormed back into the room. He stuck his head into the bathroom, saw the T-shirt and jeans she had changed into and said, "Are you wearing that?"

"I am now, but I won't be for dinner, if that's what you're asking. How was your afternoon?"

He reached over her head to grab a towel, wiping his face with it before speaking again. Claire had never seen the calm and cool Alec break a sweat before, but on him it looked good. His cheeks were flushed, and the color in his face highlighted the crystal blue of his eyes.

"First of all," he said, "I had to pursue Ms. Miranda all the way out to a cow pasture, ducking and weaving the cows' calling cards all the while. Then I still couldn't get anywhere near her to ask her a question. I got to talk to her publicist, who so graciously agreed to add our paper to the list of a thousand or so that get press releases about Miranda's movies. Then I got to talk to her personal trainer, who wanted to find out all the details of my workout routine. Then I came up against the psychic, who said that my heart was in a battle with my mind, and it would not be resolved until I let my heart win.''

"People pay a lot of money to learn that stuff," Claire said. "The day wasn't wasted, after all."

He leaned close to her as she tried to put her mascara on with a hand that was just beginning to ever so slightly shake. "I don't care about my heart," Alec whispered to her. "I care about getting Miranda to say something I can take back to my paper."

Claire recapped the mascara. Alec was standing in front of the vanity drawer, and she reached past him to try to retrieve her brush. "Do you mind?" she said. "I've got to finish getting ready."

"You'd better hurry up in here," he said. "I've got to shower and dress. You didn't happen to bring the suitcases in, did you?"

"No, just one of mine and my typewriter," she said, as he left the bathroom. "A very nice young man helped me out." She heard the door shut. "And he was very cute, too," she added, but he was gone.

EDDIE, OF EDDIE'S GARAGE and Parts Shop, was in the middle of his umpteenth explanation of how exactly Lissa's car had been totaled on the airport highway while being towed by him, Eddie, who had never had so much as a fender bender in all of his life.

"See, that merging lane right there where the Waffle House is, that's new. And some old fellow didn't realize that you're supposed to let the merging traffic merge. So there I was..."

"Merging," Lissa supplied.

"Exactly—when he just sideswiped your car, then knocked it clear off the back of my truck. The old fellow didn't have a scratch on him, thank goodness. It's just a miracle it didn't hit anybody else, either. It went into that ditch, like an eight ball heading for the pocket."

Scott, who had been faking sleep in the chair next to Lissa, sat up and winked at her. "Maybe you had to be there."

Ignoring him, Lissa said, "The important thing to me, Mr. Eddie, is that I have something to drive. When will my car be ready?"

"Oh, not till tomorrow or the next day at least."

Lissa tried to keep the panic out of her voice. "My friend and I have to get somewhere."

Eddie shrugged. "Don't know what to tell you, Miss. I'm as sorry as I can be about your car."

Lissa turned to Scott. "What do you think?"

"We could call a cab."

"Scott, do you have any idea how far we are from Loudon? A new pair of shoes or a social-occasion dress is one thing, but I can't put a hundred-dollar taxi ride on the paper's expense account." She looked at her watch. She knew Hank wouldn't have gone back home before the cook-off. "I'll get us a ride." She asked Eddie for his phone.

Hank answered on the first ring. "Hank," Lissa said.

"Lissa, is that you? Thank heavens. You've got to come immediately. All the copy's been lost, and Mick and I are trying to recreate it. Be here as soon as you can."

"I'm sorry. I must have the wrong number." She hung up and looked around the dingy garage. Outside she could see rows of cars, as though the lot were some giant auto graveyard, and Eddie, the undertaker.

"Do any of those cars run?" she asked Eddie.

He looked insulted. "Of course some of 'em run. Why just the other day, I took out that spiffy little '71 Maverick. Purred like a kitten when its exhaust pipe wasn't smoking."

Lissa turned her charm up as much as she could, considering the material she had to work with. "Mr. Eddie," she said, letting her voice rise to a feminine Southern inflection at the end. "I'm sure you aren't in the habit of lending out your valuable vehicles. But my friend and I really have to get somewhere as quickly as possible. Do you think you could maybe lend us a car?" He looked dubious, and she added quickly, "It doesn't have to be the Maverick."

"Well, I don't know. Where do you have to get that's so all-fired important?"

Figuring she owed him at least some explanation, Lissa quickly invented one. "My friend here has been engaged to my sister since they were kids, practically. He's a very important scientist, and he's been on a research trip to the rain forest. He was in the jungle when he got her Dear John letter. She's at my parents' in Loudon, and we've just got to get to her."

If she wasn't mistaken, there were tears in Eddie's eyes. Even Scott looked moved. Eddie reached into a drawer and took out a set of keys. "Go ahead," he said. "Take the Maverick. And keep it as long as it takes for her to say yes. Your car ain't going anywhere."

Wasn't that the truth, Lissa thought, as she blew Eddie a kiss and grabbed her suitcase from the trunk of her demolished car.

7

SHE WAS STILL in there. Why did every woman in the world, even one as unique as Claire, spend half her life in the bathroom? That would be an interesting topic for an exposé. He'd buy a copy of any paper willing to tackle that one.

He chose a crisp white cotton shirt and another pair of khakis—one that hadn't made the trek through the pasture. He picked out a funky-looking Art Deco tie—one his sister had bought him for Christmas. The directive was casual, but Alec didn't feel right about working without a tie. And this was work—make no mistake about it.

His clothes chosen, he sat down on the bed. Something had been bugging him about the story Claire had told him. He'd stuck to his promise not to mention it—after all, wouldn't that have been the way to get into Miranda's good graces? But he couldn't let it go.

He rummaged through his suitcase for his address book, then knocked on the bathroom door. "When are you getting out of there?"

"When I'm good and ready," she yelled back through the closed door.

He had time to make his phone call, then. He found the number for Maureen Daniels, Trent's mother, punched in his calling card number and waited for her to answer. She was the same sweet woman he remembered, crazy about her son. That was why, even though Trent Daniels's star had faded in Hollywood, Alec always made sure the paper mentioned his latest straight-to-video release.

They chatted for a few minutes, then Alec said, "Maureen, this is awkward for me to bring up, since I know you don't gossip. But it seems like Trent told me something once about Miranda Craig trying to get his attention by doing something to an actress in a play."

"It sounds crazy, doesn't it?" she asked him. "Such a sweet-looking girl. But she joked about it once to him, that she was responsible for that girl missing the play. He thought it was just fun, until he found out the girl really had gotten trapped in the mountains overnight. He asked the girl about it, but she shut up."

"Is that so?" Alec asked.

"And—" the woman lowered her voice, "—she made a pass at him, if you know what I mean. He was good enough to turn down, trying to protect her reputation."

Alec grinned. "He's a nice guy, Maureen," he told Trent's mother, hoping he sounded sincere. He glanced at the bathroom door. "Thanks, Maureen. You call me when Trent's got something new going on, okay?"

"He's filming a martial-arts movie right now." She made a clicking noise with her teeth. "Now that Miranda Craig is so big, you'd think she'd get him a part in one of her movies, but Trent says she won't even take his calls."

"It's a dirty business, Maureen," Alec told her. They hung up, and he knocked on the bathroom door again.

"Who were you talking to?" Claire asked through the door. Alec remembered again that she didn't miss much, and he decided to tell her the truth.

"I found somebody to support your story," he said. "Claire, this is great stuff."

She threw the door open, and he was greeted by a vision of beauty in red: Claire wearing a dress that was even more seductive than the white one she'd discarded. His jaw fell open, and he slapped it shut.

"I'm sorry I ever told you," she said. "I forgot what a vulture you are."

"You can't wear that," he said. "It's supposed to be casual, not barely there."

"Don't change the subject." She didn't seem upset at his criticisms. She seemed kind of triumphant, in fact. "Alec, if you'll take a good long look at this dress, you'll see that it isn't as low-cut as the white one, and it's the same length. I don't see what the problem is."

"It's so red," he said.

"So have you taken up a new career as a color consultant?" she asked. "Am I a spring, trying to pass myself off as a winter?"

No, he wanted to say. You're a timid young woman, trying to pass yourself off as a ravishing siren. And what's worse, you're succeeding. But he didn't say that. Instead, he stepped past her into the bathroom and slammed the door shut. Then he opened it again to retrieve his clothes from the bed.

"I mean it Alec," she said. "I never meant to hold her accountable for something she did years ago."

"Well," he said. "Except for that one thing she did. She's still being held accountable for that, isn't she?"

He judged that he only had a few seconds to get into the bathroom before she threw something at him. "I haven't seen you speechless in a long time, Claire. It's kind of refreshing." He shut the door and locked it.

When he got out of the shower, he could hear the heavy chink of typewriter keys, striking paper at a fast clip. Unless she was getting ready to throw the typewriter at him, this was a good sign. He hurriedly shaved and dressed, then opened the door to see Claire at the desk, a folder of notes spread out before her. She had her manual typewriter set up, and was using the fancy stationery that had been provided to them.

How many times had he seen this tableau? Claire hard at work, unaware of anyone watching her. Only that had been the shy Claire, the one who dressed in the same shades as her desk, the better to blend in with it. But here was Claire in a red dress, sitting at an ancient manual typewriter. She wore her glasses, as she usually did when she worked, and she typed at her usual steady pace. The scene was eerily familiar, yet completely different.

Finally she sensed him watching her. She didn't let out a startled scream, but rather, graced him with a smile. "You look fabulous," she said. "So clean. So rid of all traces of the cow pasture."

"Thanks," he muttered, not accustomed to accepting compliments gracefully, especially not such left-handed ones. "Did you decide to scoop me on my Miranda story?"

"I had my final interviews in south Ridgeville on the days I was away from the office, and I'm revising my piece. This way I won't get behind on my work."

"Yeah?" Alec said, picking his watch up off the dresser and snapping it on. It was 5:20. "Well, I'm already behind on my work. We've got to make sure we get to that casual dining room before anyone else."

"I hate people who are early for everything," Claire said, standing up and stretching a little.

The stretch did nothing to help him keep his mind on his work, and so he was a bit short with her when he said, "Somehow I knew that about you. Now come on."

Without further protest, Claire walked to the door and started to go out. Alec grabbed her before she could do more than stick her head out of the door.

"What are you doing?" she said loudly. He clapped a hand over her mouth and dragged her back into the room.

"We can't be seen," he said. "We can't afford to have anyone tagging along with us."

"What are you going to do? Spike the punch with truth serum so Miranda will tell all?"

"Damn, I wish I'd thought of that." He was sincere, but she kicked him in the shins anyway. "Don't mind my trick knee, Claire," he said as he rubbed it. "I injured it playing football in high school."

"Really? It's a wonder you got out of adolescence alive."

"Now," he said, ignoring her and stepping up to the door, "we're going to do this in a very systematic way. I'm going to look around the hall, and if no one is there, we're going to make a run for the stairwell."

"I think you missed your calling as a master spy," she said, but he ignored her. He looked around, and not seeing anyone, took Claire by the hand and sprinted for the stairs.

They huddled there for a second as he whispered, "Okay, the casual dining room is two doors to the right from this hallway to your left. Got that?"

She leaned against him and whispered her response, her breath tickling his ear, "When I get stressed, I have a little problem with left and right."

"Why am I not surprised?" he whispered. Sticking his head cautiously above the top of the stairs, he ducked as he saw a maid go by with a serving platter. "The maid is headed for the dining room," he told Claire in a hushed voice. "When she comes back, we'll go for it. In the meantime, if anyone comes up the stairs, we'll kiss and pretend we were stuck here in a fit of passion."

"Let's hope it doesn't come to that," Claire said.

Alec found himself disappointed that it didn't. The maid returned, sans platter, and Alec, still dragging Claire, negotiated his way through the quick left/right turns. When they got to the casual dining room, it was gloriously empty.

Alex found that his ideas of what was casual differed from those of the Craigs' decorator. Several marble-top bistro tables were set about the room, each set with service for six. Claire looked around the room, while Alec quickly went about his business, picking up his place card and setting it by Miranda's. He told Claire, "I saw the maid writing out these name cards earlier, but I couldn't get in here without anyone seeing me." He picked up the "Roger" that his card had replaced, and put it in the empty spot beside Claire's. "Roger. That doesn't sound like the name of anyone who's going to put the moves on you during dinner."

"Oh, Roger. Actually I met Roger . . ."

"Shh. Someone's coming." Alec grabbed Claire and kissed her, meaning only to continue their subterfuge for the benefit of whoever was coming into the room. Claire's muffled cry of surprise faded altogether as his arms encircled her. Suddenly, a kiss that had started out as an act became the real thing. Her lips were warm against his, and he pressed his tongue between them, meeting hers with an uncontrollable heat.

He groaned softly as her hands traveled up the length of his back. He broke the kiss off to move his lips across her neck, her fingers gripping his hair as he did so. Having never expected to feel this kind of passion around Claire, he relished the feeling all the more.

"You're so beautiful," he told her, brushing a piece of hair back from her eyes as he kissed her again. She let out a soft sigh as his hand moved up to caress her breast, but then she stopped him, and broke away from him, shaking.

No one had entered the room. "False alarm," she said.

"It felt like the real thing to me," he told her, moving toward her, needing to kiss her and feel her against him again. As his lips met hers, he heard a loud "Harumph." They broke off their kiss to see the maid standing there, shaking her head.

"Don't you all have a room?" she said.

Blushing, Claire walked around from table to table, as if looking for her place. Alec followed her. Stopping in front of her place card, she said loudly, "Gee, honey, we aren't together."

"How will we manage, sweetheart?" he asked.

"You'll get by," the maid said, leaving the room in a hurry. As she left, Claire plucked up the place card to the right of her and hurried to Alec and Miranda's table, switching it with one there.

"Stop that," Alec said. He was conscious of being all business again. "We aren't here to engage in gratuitous card-switching."

"No," she said, "but she put me next to Mrs. Schibley, who absolutely cannot stand me, and put her cousin Chris next to her so he couldn't gossip about her. I'm just righting things."

"How could this Mrs. Whoever hate you? What's not to like about you?" Alec asked, truly mystified.

She looked at him as though he'd lost his mind. "Alec, you don't like me, either."

He'd forgotten that this weekend, never more thoroughly than when he was kissing her. "I wouldn't say that," he told her. "Anyway, if I've been mean to you in the past it was because you were so absolutely innocuous."

"I can see why that would bother you," she said. "Anyway, I'm sure you'll find out why she hates me. I bet she'll lists her reasons in detail."

"Yeah?" Alec said, plopping down in his new seat. "I'm afraid I won't have time to talk to old Mrs. S. I'm going to be busy with Miranda."

Other people began to come in, most of them Miranda's relatives, and Claire made conversation with them, introducing them to Alec. Miranda's parents entered, and Alec quickly scanned the place cards around him, hoping against hope they weren't seated at their daughter's table.

Not only would it be hard for Miranda to spill her guts under the eye of her mother and father, but they would also undoubtedly notice that he wasn't exactly head table material. But who was this Roger he had replaced?

He got his answer when a lanky, familiar-looking young man strolled into the room and began looking around for his spot. Where had Alec seen him before? Was it a shampoo commercial?

The young man stood there for a second, tossing his hair back like someone striking a pose, then scratching his head a little. Oh. He was trying to look *puzzled*. Alec felt like someone caught in a low-rent game of charades.

"Roger, over here" came a melodious voice. It was Claire's. Alec twisted in his seat to see Roger stride toward the table and put his hand on Claire's shoulder.

"Great to see you again, Claire," Roger said as he plopped down in the seat beside her. How did he know Claire? And who gave him the right to strut around here like he was the next Brad Pitt?

Christine Colby and her cadre of assistants took their tables, then the rest of the Hollywood personnel filed in, their loud chatter drowning out any hopes of his eavesdropping on Claire. Not that he was interested, really. He would have plenty of conversation to monitor, once he and Miranda started talking. If she ever showed up.

He gazed anxiously around the room as Renee, Miranda's psychic, took the seat across the table from him. He met her stare for a second before breaking it off, and the look she gave him was one that said plainly, I know you don't belong at this table. He said hello to her and to Stacy, the personal trainer who'd been so impressed by his muscles earlier. She acted overjoyed to see him.

"Remember, you are going to give me all your secrets. No fair keeping any back." She turned to Renee. "This man is fabulously built."

Renee shook her head. "The body will never be happy until the intellect and the heart come together."

He thought of how his heart, body and mind had all seemed to come together smoothly when he was kissing Claire. Unable to resist a peek at her, he turned to see her laughing attractively at something Roger was saying. That Roger. What a card. He turned back to his own table, and caught a brief smirk from Renee. He resolved not to have another thought about Claire until after he escaped Renee's all-seeing, all-knowing eyes.

The table was rounded out by the appearance of Mrs. Schibley and Larry, sporting an expensive Havana cigar, which Stacy, Renee and Mrs. Schibley all loudly insisted he extinguish.

"I don't mind," Alec told him.

"Who the hell are you?" Larry asked, stubbing the cigar out in a saucer. He pointed past Alec at Mrs. Schibley. "And you?"

"I'm Alec Mason, Claire's fiancé. Remember?"

Larry had lost interest, but Mrs. Schibley perked up considerably at Claire's name. "Claire Morgan is planning to get married again? How many will this be?"

"Well, she's never been married before," Alec said.

"My point exactly," Mrs. Schibley said. "Don't you think there's something odd about a girl who gets engaged again and again, then never has the wherewithal to get married?" She pointed her finger at Alec. "She's flighty, is what she is."

That was a quality Alec hadn't attributed to Claire. Skittish, yes. That one had occurred to him. But there were other traits he hadn't noticed until this weekend. Funny. Sexy. Passionate. He was still musing over these adjectives, ignoring the retired teacher, when Miranda walked into the room.

A hush fell over the crowd. Give me a break, Alec thought to himself. Half of these people saw her every day, and as for the rest, especially the older folks, they'd seen her when she was running around in diapers. She wore a long silk cream dress with a purple floral print, and her blond hair had been swept up so that mere wisps escaped from the pins. Her makeup was laid on rather heavily, and her smile was fixed. "On behalf of myself and my parents, I want to welcome you to our family home. Eat, talk and bask in the delight of a weekend devoted to renewing old connections." The word *bask* was the only clue Alec needed to know that someone else had penned that speech for her.

She paused at Christine Colby's table before making her way to her seat, and Mrs. Schibley said, "How eloquent she's gotten. She was never that way before. Claire could write, of course."

"Did you help her with that career choice?" Alec asked.

"Ha." Mrs. Schibley cast a scornful glance Claire's way. "The girl never listened to a word I said. She always had to do things her own way."

"She's still like that," Alec told her.

"I'll bet."

Miranda finally flitted to their table, muttering to Larry, "Christine Colby is taking her job way too seriously. You promised me she wouldn't be all over me on this first night, and she has done nothing but badger me with questions. She's asked me all kinds of questions about Scott, and about my television series. She's not here to do a news piece, remind her. She's doing a tribute to me."

That seemed as good a time as any for Alec to interrupt. He said, "Miranda."

She turned toward him with all one hundred watts of her smile ablaze, but her white teeth clenched in the middle of the words "Roger, honey."

"I'm afraid not," Alec said.

"This isn't your seat," Miranda told him.

He pointed to his place card. "It's the weirdest thing, but it is. I have to admit, I thought it was odd, my being seated next to you when I'm nothing more than a huge fan and your friend's fiancé." He forced a laugh. "I just didn't want to question my good fortune."

His flattery seemed to do the trick. "That's all right, Allen," she said, peering around him to see who was beside him.

"Alec," he said, but she was focused on Mrs. Schibley, organizing her purse at the table.

"Mrs. Schibley. What a lovely surprise."

"I was invited, wasn't I?" the other woman asked.

"No, I'm sorry, I meant that I didn't realize you were at this table." She craned her neck around, and Alec watched her as her eyes went all around the room before lighting on Claire's table. There she was, sipping ice tea like it was the finest French champagne. Both Roger and Chris were hanging on her every word.

The frown lines around Miranda's eyes became more pronounced, and Alec could see her debating whether to storm over to Claire's table and jerk her wayward boyfriend and cousin back. Apparently mindful of the ever-watchful Christine Colby, Miranda turned back to the table.

Waiters came in bearing salads, as Alec tried frantically to get and keep Miranda's attention. Throughout the first course, she chewed Larry out for not chewing out her publicist about some unflattering photos that had been released the week before. During the entrée, which Alec vaguely recognized as pasta mixed with something that was not meat, she picked on her trainer for allowing her to pull a tendon in her leg during a run.

There was a brief lull while she shoveled a forkful of pasta into her mouth, and Alec took that opportunity to say, "You know, Miranda, I edit a weekly paper in Ridgeville..."

"Oh, Alex, didn't I tell my publicist to put you on her mailing list?" Miranda asked.

"Alec. Yes, you did, but I was thinking of something a little more exclusive than that."

"I'm sorry, but no. After what they said about me, it'll be a long time before I bare my soul or my talents for the Ridgeville press." She waved her fork at Alec for emphasis. "You know, it's always the hometown crowd that turns on you first. They never appreciate you, and they're all jealous of your success. What is that saying about a poet in his own town?"

"A prophet in his own country," Alec supplied. Now he knew how Claire felt around him. "But, Miranda," he said, "the *Tribune* wasn't even around then. If we had been, I'm sure we would have loved you in Chekhov. Gossip says that the only reason they panned your performance at all was that the editor's daughter had tried out for the role."

"Yes, that's true," Miranda said. She looked pleased that Alec had heard that rumor, although the truth was that he had read it in her autobiography. "But I'm so far above petty things like that now. I'm above the smallness of Ridgeville, or any kind of self-centered trivia." That said, she turned back to Larry and began haranguing him about the hairstylist they'd hired for the trip.

Alec picked at his food. He had never given up, and he wouldn't now. But this Miranda was a lot harder to crack than he'd assumed she would be.

Even if—and he wasn't yet ready to admit this was a possibility—but even if he didn't get the interview with her, he still had enough eavesdropped material to fill the inches he'd allotted for the story in this week's paper. Not to mention the anecdote Claire had shared with him, even if she had told him not to mention it.

He watched Claire's table for a second. Claire, obviously in vegetarian heaven, was digging in to her food with a hearty appetite. Roger now wore his serious face as he talked to her, and she tucked a wisp of hair behind her ear in that familiar gesture. It made him want to run back with his place card and kick Roger back to where he belonged.

"She was so stubborn. Perhaps that's why we didn't get along."

It took him a moment to figure out the remark had come from Mrs. Schibley. "I'm sorry. What did you say?"

"Claire. Quiet and stubborn. That's the worst combination, if you ask me. Bugged the hell out of me, if you'll pardon my French."

"Oh, I know what you mean," he said. He remembered Claire telling him that the woman would list all the reasons she disliked her, and with half an ear turned to Miranda and Larry, he listened for more. Even hearing bad things about Claire at least helped make her less of a mystery to him.

"She wouldn't listen. She didn't care what others thought. You know, she had just as much talent as this one," Mrs. Schibley said, pointing to Miranda, who was once again engrossed in a low-voiced argument with Larry. "But a really good actress has to want to spend her life mouthing other people's words. Claire wouldn't stand for that."

"So she acted in high school, huh?"

"In college, too." Mrs. Schibley looked again at Miranda, still ignoring them. "She took Missy's part in a play."

"Yeah, Claire mentioned that."

Mrs. Schibley leaned toward him. "The paper said, Missy Craig has shown herself to be a fine comic actress."

So why hadn't he heard about this glowing review? He'd assumed the daily had only mentioned her that once.

"But," Mrs. Schibley whispered, "the next line said, 'But it's Claire Morgan as the loopy Edna Louise who walks away with the show.'"

Ouch. For the first time, he felt the tiniest twinge of sympathy for Miranda Craig. No wonder she wanted what Claire had. He sipped his coffee thoughtfully and finished off his slice of chocolate torte. After Miranda had taken a few dainty bites of her own slice, she stood.

"Everyone, if I may have your attention, please. I want to thank you again for taking time out of your busy schedules to come here and be a part of this with me. Tomorrow, Ms. Colby and her assistants will begin interviewing you. I want you to pretend you're talking to your friends back home. If I don't like what you say, I can always edit it out later." That got a laugh from about three-quarters of the room. "Right now, I want you all to take this opportunity to get to know everyone else who's here. Again, thank you, and I love you all."

At that last line, Alec sneaked another peek at Claire. Out of the corner of his eye, he could see that Miranda, too, was staring at Roger and Claire. They were deeply absorbed in conversation. She might have gone to their table, he thought, if she hadn't been stopped by an onslaught of relatives.

"What I want to know is where was the meat?" asked one of her uncles.

"Uncle Jack, you are a regular character," Miranda said, giving the man a big hug. Alec could see that he wasn't satisfied with that answer, but Miranda moved on to the next table, still moving toward Claire and Roger. They were standing with Miranda's parents, chatting with them. Don't they make a lovely couple, Alec thought. Too lovely. And they were already a bit too friendly for his tastes. He resolved to dog Miranda's every step as she made her way toward them.

After a while, it was like some terrible dream. The closer the Miranda and Alec combination got to Claire and Roger, the farther they receded. Alec thought he should interject some word about the paper with Miranda, but he didn't have the heart. He didn't seem to have that old Alec thirst for the story. He had a thirst for Claire.

Miranda was in a conversation with an estranged aunt, and Alec was listening in, when he noticed that Claire and Roger were no longer with them. Not wanting to make Miranda ballistic by mentioning it to her, he did anyway.

"You don't see Claire anywhere, do you?"

Miranda frowned at him. "She's been with Roger all night. I'm sure they're around here somewhere, looking like they're glued at the hip." She looked around, then looked around again. "How do you like that?" she asked.

Alec didn't like it at all. Claire and Roger were nowhere to be seen, no doubt cozied up somewhere continuing their intimate dinner discussion in a more intimate setting.

"I'm sure they just went outside to get some fresh air," Alec said. With that, he and Miranda lurched toward the deck adjoining the dining room, but it was a long hard trek, filled with people who wanted to talk to Miranda. By the time they got to the deck, Claire and Roger were gone, if they had ever been there at all.

So far, the evening was a bust. Determined to wring something from this wretched night, Alec said, "Anyway, Miranda, I hope you'll think about the possibility of letting me write about you for the *Weekly Tribune*."

She put her hand to her forehead and held it there, as though her temples were throbbing, then looked around with an expression he recognized as "get this lunatic away from me." Knowing that he'd pestered her enough for one night, he couldn't resist giving it one last shot. He said, "Maybe you'd rather I write about you than Claire."

"Claire." She said it with such a combination of heartbreak and venom that he immediately felt as though he'd betrayed Claire by mentioning her name. "I have tried and tried to make up for what I did to Claire." She put her hand on her chest and said, "And you know, I did the right thing. Maybe not for the right reasons. But if she had any idea what a loser Scott turned out to be, she'd fall on her knees and kiss the ground in front of me." She shook her head so vigorously that Alec feared for the stability of her hairstyle. "Doesn't she know that I'm sorry for what I've done? How much I've wanted our friendship back? Look at her. She's walking around here in those fabulous dresses, looking more like a movie star than a movie star does. She's got a job she likes, a fiancé she loves. I didn't ruin her life forever. Why can't she forgive me?"

Miranda wasn't acting. Alec had seen most of her movies, and he knew that quite frankly, she wasn't that good. Also, she seemed dangerously near tears, and Alec didn't want to be the one caught beside her when they burst forth. He'd probably be lynched by the crowd for making her cry.

"You know what?" he said. "Claire was up late last night trying to finish some work before she left, and then we had to get up real early this morning. She never took a nap this afternoon, so I bet she's gone off to our room to sleep."

"It isn't even nine yet. And where's Roger?" Miranda asked.

"I don't know, but I'm sure they aren't together," he said soothingly. He only wished he were sure. "I'm going to slip on out and keep Claire company. I'll see you tomorrow." He waved his goodbyes to the other people who'd been at their table, then dashed out of the room and down the stairs.

He paused beside the closed door. To knock or not to knock? Claire could be in there entertaining her teen idol wannabe, and they would all be embarrassed if he simply threw the door open. On the other hand, Roger had a room, and they could jolly well go there. This was his room as well as Claire's, and a man has to sleep.

He knocked softly, then waited. Not hearing anything, he had the awful suspicion that maybe Claire had gone to

Roger's room after all. Opening the door, he glanced at the couch, then the desk. When he didn't see Claire at either of these spots, his heart sank. Then he looked at the bed.

There she was, sprawled on top of the covers, fast asleep. A magazine was beside her, and he assumed that she had come to the bed to read because the light from the lamp was better there. She'd kicked her shoes off, but she was still wearing the red dress.

He went to sit beside her. "Claire," he said into her ear. Still asleep, she rubbed the side of her head and pushed his hand away. "Claire, can you wake up and move to the couch like you promised?" He took her sleepy groan as a "no." He stood up and took his tie off. The honorable thing to do would be for him to sleep on the couch. The cruel thing to do would be for him to pick up Miss I-Never-Sleep and toss her over there. In the end, he compromised. He took a blanket from the closet, lay down beside Claire and covered them both up with it. Lying there, feeling the almost irresistible urge to hold her close, he wondered what had ever possessed him to tackle this weekend. It would have been far better for him to have stayed at the paper. Even if things didn't always run smoothly there, he was at least in control. There was no problem there that he, in his infinite smarts, couldn't handle.

"How do you spell adobo sauce?" Hank asked.

"Let's see. Sauce is *s-a-u-c-e*. Does that help?" Mick asked.

Hank took a bite out of the barbecued rib he was holding, then put it back in its take-out container. Wiping his hands on a moist towelette before going back to his keyboard, he said to Mick, "I know what you're doing. I know that you think if you don't help me, I'll let you leave. No way. Not till an adequate amount of copy is replaced."

"Hank, it's one in the morning," Mick pleaded. "Let me go home and sleep."

"I wouldn't see you the rest of the weekend. You'd go out on your boat tomorrow and forget all about the paper."

"You're a machine," Mick said.

"I remember a time when that would have been a compliment from you," Hank said, writing on.

"You know, these last few years I've been thinking that maybe there's more to life than working."

"Boating? Gambling?"

"Lots of things," Mick said. "Look at you. All you've got is your work. I'm willing to bet you don't have a single pursuit outside of what you do for this paper."

"You're wrong," Hank said.

"What is it then?"

"You'll find out someday," Hank said, getting back to his work. The spelling checker on his computer was an ancient one from the days before Yuppie food ruled the universe. It had no trace of adobo. Hank compromised on "a smoky Mexican chile sauce" and went on with his cook-off write up. Before he and Mick had allowed themselves to have a break at the barbecue, he had begun searching through Alec's notes, trying to piece together some of the stories he had written. As soon as he was finished with this, he'd continue that work. Mick's assignments were to write up the city council meeting and the wedding Lissa had left undone. Since Mick had actually been at the nuptials, Hank thought it was the least he could do.

After finishing the write-up, he glanced over at Mick. He'd fallen asleep at Lissa's desk, and was snoring a little as his head lolled over some papers. Hank let him rest. Tomorrow, he'd make sure Mick wrote something, even if he had to write it for him.

8

IF SHE WERE FOND of black, low-riding cars of the seventies, Lissa would find the Maverick acceptable. As it was, she longed for her red compact, still up on blocks at Eddie's.

"Do you know how to get to Loudon?" she asked Scott. He nodded. "Do you want to drive?"

He grinned as he took the keys from her. "The questions is, do you want me to drive? It's been a while since I've driven, since I don't have a car in New York, and I was kind of a hellion before that."

"As long as you get us there in one piece," she said. Now, barreling down the road at well over thirty miles an hour above the speed limit, she began to think that was iffy.

If the wipers had broken before she realized the car was headed in the wrong direction, she might have been okay. But when the two things happened simultaneously, her spirit broke.

"Oh, Scott," she said despondently.

He leaned toward the steering wheel and stuck a hand out the window, wiping away just a fraction of the rain on the windshield. "We haven't known each other long enough for me to have caused that tone of disappointment." He stuck his soaking arm out again. "Damn, this isn't helping."

"You told me you knew how to get to Loudon. You're going the wrong way."

"That's not possible," he said.

"Scott, we're forty miles on the other side of the lake from where we're supposed to be."

He slowed the car down a little, keeping up his impromptu wiping. "What makes you think so?"

"This is west Ridgeville. This is not Loudon. I know because our publisher, Mick Regan, has our Christmas and summer parties in his house on the lake, which is about a half mile from here."

Scott shook his head, seemingly amazed at himself. "You know what? This is the way to Claire's grandparents' house. We used to come down to the park then take a boat to Loudon." He shook his head. "The subconscious is a tricky thing."

"My subconscious usually has the decency not to fool me into driving halfway across the state," Lissa said. "Yours must not like you."

Before he had a chance to respond, the skies opened for real, and the steady rain turned into a tremendous downpour. Thunder boomed, and although Lissa hadn't seen any lightning, it was loud enough to make her wonder if the fireworks were headed their way.

Scott hadn't made an attempt to turn around, and she saw Mick's driveway coming up on their left. "Pull in here," she ordered.

"Here?"

"Now," she said. He turned the wheel quickly, and they slid into the driveway, taking out Mick's mailbox on the way. Feeling she'd been a little harsh with Scott, she put a hand on his arm and said, "Don't worry. He can afford to buy another one."

"What are we going to do here?"

"We're going to sit and drink coffee with Mick till the storm passes. Then we'll head out again."

They got out of the car, the wind whipping Lissa's hair into an uncontrollable rat's nest, and the hard drops of rain stinging her face. They dashed for the covered porch.

Lissa pounded on the front door. "He's got to be here."

Scott moved past her and rang the doorbell. "Maybe this will help, although it isn't as dramatic as trying to beat down the door."

She would have rebuked him, except that just then she felt electricity in the air and saw lightning crack across the way. The thunder was only a second behind. "Whether he's here or not, we've got to get in," she said. "He leaves a key around here somewhere for his kids. Help me look." Scott went through the planter while Lissa shook out the welcome mat. As he poked around the windowsills, Lissa unearthed the key under a large rock in the flower bed. They got the door open as lightning hit nearby and thunder shook the whole house.

CLAIRE HATED thunderstorms. Let Alec go on about property values all he wanted to, but that was one disadvantage of living on the lake. The storms blew harder over the water, and there were many nights when she held her breath until sunrise, waiting on the next roll of thunder.

So when this one hit while she slept, she woke for a second, startled, but then fell back to sleep. She had the sensation that someone was here to protect her from harm.

She would have dismissed it as a middle-of-the-night fancy if she hadn't awakened the next morning to feel strong arms around her, to feel herself being held close. Her eyes still closed, she rolled over to bury her face in the hard chest of her protector. Still half dreaming, she took a deep breath and breathed in the clean, fresh scent of Alec.

Alec? Claire sat up in a hurry, throwing the blanket off of both of them and giving Alec a good hard shake. She took a good look at him, happy to see that he'd slept in his cotton shirt, now a wrinkled mess, and his khakis, also in bad need of ironing. She, at least, was still wearing her red dress. Alec hadn't responded to her shake, so she did it again, this time with more vigor.

"What? What is it?" he asked, rubbing his eyes. He opened them and looked at her. "Oh, hey, Claire," he said, taking her hand. "How did you sleep?"

She dropped his hand as though it were a wet fish. "Don't you 'Hey, Claire, how did you sleep?' me. I want to know how you wound up in this bed."

He sat up. "So it's that kind of day, is it? I want to know how you came to be sleeping in this bed when you volunteered for the couch."

Claire thought. She remembered Roger walking her back to her room, but she hadn't invited him in. She'd had this idea she could get some work done on her story, but instead, she'd picked up a magazine and started reading it on the bed, where the light was better. Since she didn't remember anything of the story she was supposed to be reading, she guessed that she had nodded off right away. She hadn't meant to steal the bed from Alec, but that was no excuse for his sleeping with her.

"I fell asleep reading," she said.

"Yes, that magazine and your dress were convenient props."

"It was an accident. You should have done the decent thing and slept on the couch."

"That's exactly what you meant for me to do."

She walked the few steps to the couch, then collapsed there. Even though she'd slept better than she had in a long time, she now felt cross and out of sorts, probably because of the shock she'd received upon awakening. She hadn't even had time to daydream about and relive the kiss they'd shared the night before, when she'd woken up to find herself in Alec's arms. Even worse, she'd had to force herself to remember that she didn't belong there.

After getting up to retrieve the magazine from the bed, she sat back down with it, trying to read the same story she'd intended to read last night. Putting it aside for a second, she said, "Don't worry. You can have the bed tonight." She began reading again.

"Oh, sure. That's what you said yesterday."

She threw the magazine down. "Are you mad about the bed or is there more?"

"More. For one thing, there's that shy-little-mouse act you've perpetrated for the four months you've worked for the paper, when all along you were ready to throw on a red dress and play the femme fatale."

"You really hate this color, don't you?"

Alec scooted across the bed and threw himself on the couch next to her. "It's not that. I want to know why the you I see here is so different from the you I know."

Because you don't know me, she wanted to say. Because from the first second I saw you, I've been a hopeless and tongue-tied mess. Because I'm pretending to be more confident than I am. But she didn't say any of those things. Instead, she said, "I don't know what you're talking about."

"Your fiancés, for example. How did you get this football team full of men who wanted to marry you?"

"It wasn't a football team's worth." She began ticking them off on her fingers. "There was Brad, who actually was a football player. I felt obligated to go out with him because he'd dumped the head cheerleader for me. I dated him for about a year in high school, but I got worried when he started talking about marrying me before he went to college so I could write his papers for him."

"Who else?" Alec demanded.

"Brian, who was a sensitive artist type, and who threatened to throw himself in a vat of paint if I ever left him. He lived. And in the first year of college, Rick, who was my biology TA. There was also Russ, who went out with me twice then bought me a ring, but I don't count him because his parents had him institutionalized shortly thereafter."

"And Scott," Alec said softly.

She was surprised that the name only caused a fraction of the pain she had felt when she heard it just a week ago. "And Scott."

"I noticed Roger couldn't stop himself from fawning over you at dinner last night."

Claire smiled. Alec actually sounded jealous.

"Roger is crazy about Miranda. I wouldn't say he was fawning," Claire said.

"I'm surprised he had enough polysyllabic words in his vocabulary to keep his end of the dinner chat up that long."

"Another misjudgment on your part," Claire said. "Roger happens to be a really bright guy, and we were having an interesting conversation."

"An interesting conversation?" he scoffed. "Everyone in the room thought you would duck out before dessert was served."

"Take that back," she said. A flattering interest in her affairs was one thing, but not outright slander.

"I'm sorry, but it's true," he said. "I don't know how you could have let him make such a play for you, after that kiss."

That kiss. Her heart jumped, and her pulse started pounding, remembering that kiss. The way his lips had felt, the strong feel of his body pressed against hers. But the kiss was an act, part of the farce they were perpetuating throughout the weekend. Had he forgotten that? Or, more likely, was he using her attraction to him as a way of manipulating her?

"That kiss wasn't real, Alec."

He looked hurt, only it was a genuine hurt, not the kind of mock-pouting he did when he was trying to talk her into some despised task. "It was real," he said. "You felt what I felt."

"But that has nothing to do with us, with who we are and what we're here for. That kiss was about as real as this sapphire. The stone's genuine, but the story behind it isn't." She grabbed a suitcase, and took off into the bathroom. "I've got to meet Christine Colby after breakfast."

She showered, blew her hair dry and dressed. The word for the interviews was "look as though you're going on a picnic." For a normal picnic, she'd probably throw on a pair of oversize shorts and a giant T-shirt—either that, or one of those dresses that resembled a caftan. For this day, she put on a neatly pressed pair of khakis and a white sleeveless blouse, one that buttoned up the front.

If she expected to find Alec in a better mood when she emerged from the bathroom, she'd been engaging in wishful thinking. He was reading her magazine and sulking on the bed. "Thank goodness I don't have to share a bathroom with you all the time," he said. "I'd never get to work. As it is, I'm running late."

"Yes, I could tell that Miranda was very eager to talk to you." Ouch. That was a cruel cut, and she hadn't really meant to say it.

He rebounded quicker than she thought he would. "I guess she'll be eager to talk to me when she finds out that you haven't been able to keep your mouth shut about her youthful indiscretions. Isn't that just the kind of vengeful story a jilted ex-friend would spread?"

Claire smiled. "Except that's it true. And you're the one who's petty enough to bring it up."

"People ought to be able to account for their actions, don't you think?"

"It means nothing to me," Claire said. "I don't have any skeletons in my closet to rattle."

"Are you sure about that?" Alec asked. "Mrs. Schibley said you, not Miranda, were the hit of that play. Didn't Trent Daniels notice you?"

She grinned. "You're guessing. And you're wrong. I didn't need Trent Daniels. I had Scott, remember?" She turned the knob. "Besides, he just didn't seem like the kind of guy who'd propose on the first date."

With that, she left the room. When she stepped outside the house, she was pleased to discover that it was a beautiful, bright day. The storm of the night before had cooled the air down, and left some debris on the sidewalk, but all other traces of it were gone. Everyone was clustered around a breakfast buffet by the pool, most of them fighting and pawing over the danishes and pastries at the end of the table. Reluctant to enter the fray, Claire took a cup of fruit salad and a small container of yogurt, and sat down by Chris in a chair next to the pool.

Christine Colby walked through, trailed by a cadre of assistants and cameramen. "The friend, the friend. I want to start with the friend."

Claire waved a hand. "Here I am."

Christine stopped in front of her. "Are you finished eating yet, sweetie? We've got to hurry."

Claire nodded and stood, throwing her things away in a nearby wastebasket. "Okay, people," Christine yelled as she passed. "Some of you don't look dressed," she said, as the relatives looked down, puzzled, at their bathing suits and jogging shorts. "Be ready when we call for you, okay?"

Christine and Claire walked down past the pool, down into the pasture. Christine looked as classy walking through the Craigs' farmland as she did on her television specials. "Watch your step," she said. "This is a working pasture."

"That's what I heard," Claire told her. "Where are we headed?"

"There's a run-down barn over this hill. It isn't the one the Craigs use for their cows, so we turned it into a temporary headquarters. I've got some bales of hay for you to sit on while you talk to me, then I think Miranda might join us for a shot on the swing in the gazebo nearby."

Claire wasn't looking forward to taping an intimate talk with Miranda. Her feelings about her friend were too mixed-up to come out coherently. It was awful to have a friend you couldn't trust, but in some ways it was worse not to have that friend at all. There were times when she missed the sparkle Miranda had put into her life. She knew she needed people in her life who liked to live for the moment. Scott had been like that, as were Allie and Lissa. And Alec, Claire thought to herself. Alec seems like someone who seizes the day the second the alarm clock rings.

Claire followed Christine into the barn. Several cameras had been set up in there, and lights blared at her from all directions. Christine shielded her eyes. "Tone it down a little, guys."

An area had been cleared out for the makeup woman and hairstylist, and Christine shooed Claire off in their direction. "Hurry up with her," she said. "We've got to get rolling. I think her hair is fine, but do her face up brighter."

Claire wanted to protest, but she didn't. After an expert application of blush and eyeliner, she was sent back to the bale of hay, where Christine was perched in a chair across from her. "I know you feel like you're wearing a lot of makeup," Christine said, "but you won't look washed-out this way. Here's what we're going to do. I'm going to sit here and talk to you for a second, then we're going to turn the cameras on and talk about Miranda."

Christine Colby was one of Claire's favorite newspeople, even though Claire had never had any interest in doing broadcasting. And although Claire wanted to move from life-style features to hard news, Christine Colby had done the opposite, moving from a network correspondent's position to being able to host her own one-hour specials on celebrities and public figures of her choice.

"Where do you live, Claire?" Christine asked her.

"I live in Ridgeville, in a house my grandfather built for my parents when they were newlyweds." The familiar story, almost her own kind of fairy tale, calmed her out of her nervous state, and she and Christine chatted about her time in school as an English major and her career as a reporter.

"All right," Christine said, "we're going to start rolling the tape now. You're doing great.

"How did you meet Miranda?" she asked.

"It was the third week of first grade, and Missy, as I knew her then..." She remembered that the Missy/Miranda question of yesterday had never been settled, but at Christine's nod, she went on. "...Missy had just been kicked out of Miss Talley's class for making faces at the teacher. She came to my first-grade class, sat down beside me and offered me a piece of bubble gum, which we weren't allowed to have. We were friends from then on."

Christine led her through more memories of Miranda, including their first school play. "We were elves in this Christmas pageant, but our mothers didn't finish our long caps until right before the show. No one thought to stuff them with newspaper to make them stand up on our heads, so they kept dangling in front of our eyes. The whole house was howling at us, and we were so proud, because someone had told us it was a comedy and that we were supposed to make people laugh."

The trip down memory lane veered into more recent territory. A high school field trip, when the back end of the bus had fallen through a wooden bridge and Claire had helped a hysterical Miranda disembark. A high school production of *The Importance of Being Earnest,* with the two of them in the young female leads. College, when the two of them were roommates and Claire had run lines with Miranda, helping her learn her parts.

Claire was thinking that she'd gotten off pretty easily when Christine said, "Do you ever look at your friend's glamorous life and think What if that were me? Is that something you wanted for yourself? Do you ever think Why am I still stuck in Ridgeville?"

Although she'd done a lot of soul-searching about her relationship with Miranda, she didn't have a ready answer. Slowly she began to talk. "I think it's wrong to want to be famous for the sake of being famous. In Miranda's work, celebrity is the goal. In my work as a reporter, I almost think invisibility is the goal. If I can help somebody out by staying behind the scenes and writing my copy, that's what I want to do."

"In Ridgeville?" Christine asked.

"I came back to Ridgeville by choice," Claire said. Although she knew Miranda wanted the subject of Scott to be off-limits, it was important to her that she be able to finish what she had to say. "My fiancé, Scott Granville, used to talk all the time about moving to New York. He believed that was the only place he could make his mark as a novelist. I argued and resisted, until one day he went to New York with Miranda. When that happened, I did leave Ridgeville, although not for New York. But when I came back, I knew I was at peace with being there."

Claire could tell that Christine was grateful to her for sparing her the dirty task of introducing Scott's name into the conversation. "A lot was said in the press at one time about Miranda's betrayal of you. Do you forgive her now?"

"Yes, I do," she answered, and as she said it, she realized she meant it. "I can't deny that part of the reason I forgive her is that I no longer have feelings for Scott. If I were still pining away for him, I don't think I'd be here."

Saying it, she realized that was true, as well. No matter how unwilling she had been to come here, how many twinges of pain she'd felt at his name, it wasn't the same as that wild and sick loneliness she'd endured when he left. If she'd still felt that, nothing would have made her see Miranda again. "My relationship with him didn't work out. He and Miranda didn't work out. There's no sense in anyone remaining bitter about that. Wherever he is, I wish him luck."

That was a wrap. She found herself shaking a little when Christine cued the cameras to stop. "I know that was hard for you," Christine said. "You were wonderful."

Claire got up and brushed some clinging hay from her pants. An assistant had retrieved Chris for his turn at the camera, and Claire considered hanging around to see what mischief he would pull. Instead, she decided she'd head back to her room and finish the south Ridgeville story. She hadn't acquired the typewriter just to use as an interesting paperweight. Walking out of the barn, past the glaring lights, she bumped into Alec, standing by the door.

"You did great," Alec said. "You've got a great camera presence. And the way you talked, it all sounded so believable."

"The truth usually does," Claire said.

Alec's jaw tensed. He stood in front of her, trying to block her path as people milled about them, going to and from the barn. He seemed to forget that they were in the great outdoors, not trapped in the office or in their room. She sidestepped him easily, but he grabbed her arm. "I came up here to apologize," he said. "I didn't mean for our argument to get so out of hand, and I didn't mean to hint anything about you and Trent Daniels." He paused to take a deep breath, and she knew then that getting that apology out had been difficult for him. "Also, I meant to tell you. You look beautiful today."

"You don't have to get carried away," she said. She twirled a piece of hair around her finger, and was shocked into silence when Alec reached up to tuck the stray lock behind her ear. "You know, that used to drive me crazy, the way you played with your hair. It still does, but in a different way." He leaned over and kissed her, a sweet brush on the lips. She heard one of Miranda's cousins yell "Public Display of Affection!", and she broke off the kiss, blushing.

"Whose benefit was that for?" she asked him.

"No one but mine and yours," he said. "Did you mean what you said about being over Scott?"

"Of course I did," she said, looking straight at him. He wore another one of his polo shirts, this one red, but he had on jeans, tight in all the right places. That first day she had seen him on the elevator, she'd thought no man could be that gorgeous, but he looked even better today than he had all those months ago.

"But that was the whole reason you didn't want to come here, remember?"

She took his hand and steered him under the shade of a nearby tree. "You can be sad about something and still think that it turned out okay in the long run. I was upset because of Scott, of course, but also because the whole thing told me something I didn't want to know about Miranda. Or Scott. I didn't want to think the people I loved could be that shallow."

"But you wanted to marry Scott," Alec said stubbornly.

Claire laughed. "There are a lot of people here who would tell you that doesn't put him in a very select category. But let me try to explain." They sat down on a nearby rock. "Those guys before Scott..."

"Brad, Brian, Rick and Russ," Alec interrupted.

"You remembered," she said, pleased in spite of herself. "These guys, who wouldn't take 'I won't marry you' for an answer, didn't fall in love with the real me. I can be sweet, sure, but as you know, I can also be pretty darn sour."

"And sharp-tongued," Alec said.

"That, too," she admitted. "When Scott and I started dating, I thought he loved me for the real me. And maybe that was true. But he didn't love the real me enough to give up the chance to go to New York with Miranda."

"What if you had gone to New York with him instead of Miranda?" Alec asked.

"I can't say," she said. "I don't know if we'd still be together, and I don't know that he would have written any more novels with me than he wrote with her."

"What about you, though?" Alec asked. "What would you be doing?"

"I think I would have still found my calling. I think journalism is what I was meant to do. When my front of the paper stories start coming out, I want to be able to see that they really have meaning for the people I write about."

"You really believe that what you write matters?" Alec asked.

"Don't you?" He looked so uncomfortable and stricken by the question that she moved on to something else. "Thanks to Miranda's book, you know all the secrets of my love life. I know you dated Lissa, but who else?"

He seemed honestly shocked. "How did you know about that?"

"She told me."

"And I thought you didn't gossip."

"I don't gossip," she said, squeezing his arm. "I just listen very well. She never told me about anyone else you dated, though, so tell me about all the old loves out there pining away for you."

He cupped her chin with his hand and stroked her cheek with his thumb. "I've never met anyone I wanted to get serious about. I guess I never realized what I was looking for."

"And what's that?" she asked, half out of breath from his light touch.

"Someone who gets under my skin," he said. "Someone who keeps me off balance. Someone who surprises me."

He bent toward her, as though he were going to give her another one of those marvelous kisses, but suddenly stopped and gestured to the land nearest the house. "See that little dot in the sun hat?" he asked Claire, straightening up.

She shook her head. "Not really," she said, squinting at the distance.

"It's Miranda. Listen, I've got to get her to talk to me. This is great. I brought my tape recorder with me," he said, patting his pocket as he stood. Claire pulled him back down.

"Alec," she said, "we're having a meaningful discussion here. I don't think this is exactly the time for you to rush off, chasing Miranda."

"Claire, I'd love to hang out with you all day. But this story is going in the next issue. That's just days away," he said.

"Oh, I forgot," she said, knowing she was going to sound hateful but unable to stop herself. "Ridgeville residents don't buy enough copies of the *National Enquirer* to be able to figure out what Miranda's up to now."

His face darkened. "If that person in the sun hat were a company executive dumping toxic waste in south Ridgeville, you'd be the one running down the hill."

"That's different," Claire said.

"Why? Because *Weekly Tribune* readers care a lot more about industrial bad guys than they do about blond actresses? I don't think you know your reader very well."

"I don't think you do," Claire said. The set of his jaw made it clear she had angered him, and she went on, making an attempt to smooth over what she'd said. "I think if you'd give the people some real journalism, they'd want even more of it. I don't disapprove of you trying to get this story about Miranda. I disapprove of you acting like it's the most important story you'll ever write."

So much for smoothing things over. Alec grabbed his tape recorder and took a few steps away from her. "When you get down off your ethical high horse, let me know," he said.

"I'll get down from my high horse the day you become a little less . . ." She paused, knowing she shouldn't say it. "Shallow," she finished, and watched as he tightened his shoulders before walking down the hill toward Miranda.

9

"THE SUN IS SHINING, and it's a beautiful morning. It's a day that just calls out, Mick. Why don't you write about the recent city council meeting and that distinguished wedding you attended?"

Mick lifted his head off Lissa's desk and glared at Hank. He said, "Coffee," and Hank put a steaming cup down on the desk across from him.

Mick looked outside at the clear day. "Was there a thunderstorm last night or was that one of the nightmares that came from sleeping with my head crooked?"

"No, it was real," Hank said. "I had to shut the computers off and work on Alec's stories by hand, but I got a couple of them re-created and entered into the computer this morning. By looking at the assignment sheet, I've also been able to put back together a few of Lissa's stories. She left names in her notebook, and her stories are all the same anyway." Together he and Mick said, "I went to a wedding, the food was okay, the women were pleasant and the bride was pale."

Mick nodded. "Sounds like you've got the formula down pat at least. How about writing my stories?"

"No can do." Hank sat down at his computer. "Tell me all about that city council meeting. You talk, and I'll type."

"Let's see," Mick said. "I went to the municipal building. I looked around to see if there was anyone there I wanted to avoid...."

"WAKE UP. The sun's out. We're free to go." Not sure where she was or who was addressing her, Lissa opened her eyes to see an incredibly good-looking man looming over her. Who was he? More importantly, would he someday inherit a thriving manufacturing plant or palatial estate?

She sat up and looked around. This looked like Mick's house. It was Mick's house. The whole thing came back to her and woke her up in a matter of seconds. Scott. Cute he might be, but in the end, she told herself, way too much trouble to justify. Unless, of course, he had a lot of money. She hadn't had an occasion to ask him about that yet.

"Is there coffee?" she yawned.

"Great coffee. Your friend has taste."

"Mick?" She shook her head. "No, he doesn't. Isn't he here yet?"

"Nobody but you and me. I hope nothing happened to him." At Lissa's questioning glance he said, "Because you'd be upset."

"That's sweet of you," she said, genuinely touched. "But I'd get over it, really." Privately she wondered where this altruistic streak had come from. And why was he in such a bouncy mood? He'd even brought her suitcase up from the car. As she toddled off to get ready, cup of coffee in hand, she wondered if Scott's good mood had to do with the prospect of winning Claire back. For the first time, she considered the idea that she might be just setting him up for heartbreak, and was surprised to find herself bothered by the idea.

They locked up the house and hid the key in the same spot. Scott behind the wheel, they tore out of the driveway, flying past the downed mailbox at the bottom.

Near the end of Mick's road, she saw a man holding up a sign that said Slow.

"Whoa," she and Scott yelled at once, as he put the brakes on quickly. The car lurched, spun a little, then spun back as they came to a stop just a few feet shy of a mammoth tree lying across the road.

The power tools the men were using didn't seem to be making a dent in its hundreds-of-years-old flesh. Lissa and Scott got out and approached a man standing to the side of the work.

"You'd better watch your speedometer, son," the man said. "Ivy's grown over the speed limit signs, but it's thirty miles an hour around here."

Scott ignored the man's admonishments. "How long's it going to take to get this out of the way?"

"All day I guess."

"We need to get to Loudon," Lissa said. "Can you tell us how to do that?"

"Wait for the tree to get cut up," the man said. "This is a dead-end road."

"No," Lissa said, her cry one of agony. "We can't."

"If you had a boat, you could get there that way."

Scott was shaking his head in disgust, but Lissa said, "A boat? We have a boat."

"We do?" Scott asked.

Lissa bobbed her head up and down. "Back at the house. A pontoon boat. One of those flat party boats. We'll be in Loudon in no time."

"Not ten minutes from here by water," the man agreed. Scott and Lissa got back into the car. "The speed limit," the man yelled after them, as Scott floored it on the way back to Mick's.

THE LUNCH BUFFET was set up inside, in the casual dining room. The fruit and yogurt she'd had earlier didn't have much staying power, and Claire's stomach rumbled as she walked into the house, intending to grab a sandwich and take it back to her desk. With Alec out of the way, maybe she could get some work done. She ignored the voice that told her she'd rather have Alec tucked away beside her than all the sandwiches and typewriters in the world. Looking at the spot where she and Alec had kissed the night before, she felt a hunger and an ache that had nothing to do with the food set out on the buffet table.

"I'm glad you made it." She turned to see Roger standing beside her. "I hate to eat alone."

A bit flustered, Claire said, "Oh, I wasn't going to eat here. I've got some work to do in my room."

He gave her that dazzling cinematic smile. "You can't take fifteen minutes to sit at a table and eat with me?"

Her plate full, he steered her toward a seat. "You don't know how nice it feels to talk to somebody who knows something about the world outside of Hollywood."

"Have you gotten to see a lot of Miranda this weekend?" she asked him.

He shook his head. "No, I've barely been able to say two words to her. When she gets involved in something, she goes all out after it."

"Believe me, I knew that too well," Claire said.

Roger blushed. "I didn't have to bring up what happened between you and Miranda. You know, she wouldn't have invited you if she hadn't thought that maybe you two could still be friends somehow."

"Do you think so?" Claire asked, interested. Friends with Miranda. That was something she hadn't seriously considered when she'd packed her three suitcases for this trip. She'd never dreamed there would be a day when she could look at Miranda without seeing a ghost image of Scott standing beside her. This weekend, though, she was having a hard time remembering exactly what Scott looked like.

There was no denying that there were things about Miranda that had always fascinated her. Miranda had had a sense of personal style from the day she started mismatching her socks at age six. She'd never hesitated with a wisecrack or joke, even if it meant ticking off someone

important. She was the first one to say "get lost" to a
group of annoying guys at a bar, even as Claire had decided to suffer their company in silence. Claire would have
probably been engaged to a whole other cast of losers if
Miranda hadn't been there to stand up for her.

But she had her faults, too. She'd never cared how her
actions affected other people. She envied things—everything from Starr McCoy's "Charlie's Angels" lunch box
to their college suitemate's candy red convertible. And she
had minimal impulse control.

This is not a woman who would be very understanding
if she caught you out with her boyfriend. "Are you sure
Miranda won't mind if she sees us eating together?" Claire
asked.

"Don't be silly," Roger said. "Miranda wants me to
make sure you have a good time on this trip, considering
that you have every reason in the world not to be here."

"Did she tell you that?" Claire asked.

"Not exactly," Roger said. "But I know she's thinking
it."

Just then, Claire heard an unfamiliar voice say, "How
did you get rid of that reporter?" Eavesdropping was one
of her best tricks in trade, and she'd developed an uncon-
scious habit of tapping into conversations around her just
long enough to figure out whether she needed to hear them
or not.

The question was answered by Miranda, walking into
the room as she spoke. "I told him to meet me by the frog
pond. He's cute, but, man, is he a pest."

Roger's back was to Miranda, and if he had heard her
enter the room at all, he hadn't let on. There was nothing
to do except pretend that she didn't know Miranda was in
the room until the actress actually ventured to their table.

Claire looked up when Miranda tapped a long finger-
nail on their table. "Hey, Miranda. How are you?"

Her smile was tight. "Did the two of you have a nice lunch?"

Claire groaned theatrically. "I can't believe how wonderful this food is, Miranda. It's so nice of you to feed us so well."

Miranda looked down her nose at the remnants of the sandwich on Claire's plate. "Claire, you had pimiento cheese."

"But it was your mother's homemade pimiento, wasn't it?" Claire asked, praying that it was.

"Well, yes," Miranda admitted, plopping down in the seat next to Roger, who leaned over and gave her a kiss on the cheek. It didn't seem to placate her.

"I can always tell the difference," Claire said. She put her napkin down on the plate and started to stand up.

"Don't go on my account," Miranda said, accepting a plate from her personal trainer and frowning at its contents.

"Oh, I'm not," Claire said, unable to believe how nervous she was in front of her old friend. This was the Miranda she'd had to comfort after she'd been laughed out of the changing room in seventh-grade gym class for being the only one who still didn't wear a bra. This was the Miranda who had called Claire the morning after she'd spent the night with Trent Daniels. There was nothing Miranda could do to her. Except steal Alec, a warning voice said. Ridiculous. Alec wasn't Claire's to steal.

"I'll give you guys some time alone," Claire said.

"Christine is going to want to interview the two of us together sometime," Miranda said. "I'm afraid we're behind schedule, so I don't know exactly when it will be."

"You know where to find me," Claire said.

She left, wondering if she should go retrieve Alec from his lonely post at the frog pond. She decided that he could take care of himself. Besides, it wasn't like he hadn't abandoned her, midkiss, to chase after Miranda. Let him

grow moss-covered down by the water. She really did have
work to do.

SINCE ALEC HAD HEARD a great deal on the news about an
apparent worldwide shortage of frogs, he thought he
should bring all those alarmed scientists down to the
Craigs' pond, where he had just spent at least half an hour
being tormented by the amphibians' croaks. Every "rib-
bit" was designed to sound like "idiot." He was surrounded by a crowd of critics, all telling him what he
already knew. Claire didn't respect him, and Miranda was
playing him for a fool.

Passing the time with the pondside crowd had given him
plenty of opportunities to brood about his argument with
Claire. Last week, he would have had a good laugh at the
expense of anyone who'd asked him whether it was possible that he and Claire could ever be right for each other.
This past day and a half, though, had made that possibility not only realistic but tempting. Now he was back to the
divide that had existed between them earlier.

He was the kind of guy who wanted to bulldoze farms
for upscale housing developments, and she was the kind of
girl who encouraged the commonfolk to lie down in front
of the bulldozers. He was all flash and style, and she was
nothing if not rock-solid substance wrapped up in deceptive packaging. She was all integrity. He was, as she'd said,
shallow.

He plopped down on a grassy spot on the bank. He
hadn't always been shallow, he told himself in his own defense. Claire only thought that because she was new to this
business. She was still at that neophyte save-the-world
stage. She didn't know yet how quickly her ambitions
would whither, how skeptical she would become about any
story that didn't arrive via fax machine or as a result of
drinks with some political insiders at the local bar. Although Alec had once wanted to turn the town on its ear

with the paper, he was now content simply to make less spelling and grammar errors than the daily. When exactly had that happened? he wondered.

"I'm so glad you're still here," he heard someone yell. He looked up to see Miranda flying down the hill toward him. She looked like a commercial—in fact, during her early days, hadn't she played in a commercial in almost this setting? Lavender-scented soap, he recalled. He stood, and she reached him at last and took him by the arm.

"You won't believe the trouble I had getting away from everybody at the house. And all the time I was thinking, Alec's at the frog pond, and he's going to think I was trying to stand him up." The corners of her mouth turned down a little. "Please say you forgive me."

"Of course," he said. The scientists also talked about the hallucinogenic properties of some frogs. Had he caught some of that in the air, or was Miranda really apologizing to him?

She went on. "I've been thinking about what you said about how the *Weekly Tribune* wasn't around when I played Elena in *Uncle Vanya,* and that it's not really fair to punish you for what the daily did."

"Right," Alec said. "Plus, this would be one way of maybe getting back at them. They know that you're never going to give them an interview—for good reason, of course. They'd hate it if they saw that you had decided to take your story to us."

Miranda was nodding thoughtfully. "You're right, you know. I don't have to be anywhere for a couple of hours. Is this a good time for you?"

"Perfect," Alec said. He couldn't understand his good fortune, although he was trying not to question it. But the only explanation he could think of was that the kind things Claire had said about Miranda had softened her up.

He switched his tape recorder on, and they chatted as they walked toward the lake. Alec clarified the basics of what he knew about Miranda's career, while trying not to duplicate questions he knew she'd been asked many times before. They sat down on the pier beside the lake, and Miranda slipped her shoes off, dangling her feet off the pier toward the water. Alec remembered that he had dreamed about this moment, Miranda confiding to him at lakeside. But as he looked off toward the shore, all he could think of was Claire. Did she ever sit on the bank of her lake? What went through her head when she was there?

"What are you thinking about?" Miranda asked him.

Alec came back to earth and grinned at Miranda. "I'm supposed to be interviewing you, not the other way around." He ran through some possible answers that didn't involve Claire. "I was wondering if you ever miss sitting beside this lake when you're in California or New York."

"I miss it a lot, actually," she confided. "It's funny—as soon as I had the money, I built this house for my parents so they could go fishing. I always say it's my home, too, but that's the kind of thing I left Tennessee to escape. Now, sometimes when I'm eating lunch at some really trendy place, I wish I was sitting here with a bologna sandwich."

Alec took a good look at her. She seemed sincere. She continued, "I'm not saying I'm sorry I left. I like what I do, and I wouldn't want to work in some office or some restaurant. I didn't really have any other plans."

Alec restrained himself from filling the silence, wanting to give Miranda a chance to share more of her thoughts. Instead, she asked him another question. "What about you? Did you want to do something besides be the editor of the *Tribune*?"

"You mean like write a novel or something?" In fact, he had no burning desire to write a novel, which made him stand out from almost every other reporter and editor he'd ever known. But that's what people seemed to accept as the secret desire of the newsman.

Her eyes widened. "Oh, goodness, no. I've had it up to here with novel writers. That's what Scott was."

"Right. I forgot," he said. He wondered if Scott was more likely to write his novel than any of the newsmen he knew. Probably not, he decided, glad to think the worst of Scott.

"No, I mean something else. Or doing what you do somewhere else."

"I did do something else," he said. Always careful not to share any of himself with his subjects, Alec wondered what he was doing chatting so intimately with Miranda Craig. It was the thing with Claire, he knew, that had left him off kilter. "I wanted to be a big-city reporter, so I left for Atlanta when I got out of school. I really loved it, too. Then Mick Regan, my favorite professor, called. He wanted to start a weekly paper with some money he'd inherited. He was eventually going to take it twice-weekly, then daily. He made the whole thing sound so exciting that I quit and drove on up that night."

"Has it been exciting?" Miranda asked.

"In some ways," he told her. Maybe not as exciting as it could have been if he'd gotten out of the office and chased a real story once in a while.

Alec steered the conversation back to Miranda, and the two talked until it was time to switch sides on the ninety-minute tape. He had another tape stashed in his other pocket, just in case he needed it.

"I really appreciate you changing your mind about this interview," he told her.

Miranda, he thought, looked almost guilty. "I should tell you . . ." she started to say, then stopped.

"Tell me what?"

She gave him a bright smile. "That I'm ready to talk some more."

HALFWAY INTO the recitation of his experiences at the city
council meeting, Mick realized that Hank's slow and me-
thodical typing was not the best way to convey all that he
had burning in his heart.

"Give me that damn machine," he said, wresting control of the keyboard away from Hank. Mick surprised
himself by remembering, almost verbatim, what had been
said and done at the meeting. But more importantly, he
emphasized in his article that the same goofballs were
saying and doing the same stupid things they'd been doing since he last attended a meeting decades ago.

He carefully saved the article on a disk, just so there'd
be no room for mistakes. "You've got to read this right
away," he bellowed at Hank, but when he looked up at the
reporter, he'd fallen asleep in his chair. Mick considered
taking his hat and tiptoeing out of the office.

He half rose from his chair, then sat back down again.
Starting a new, untitled file in the word processing pro-
gram, he told himself he'd leave after he finished one
thing. He was going to give that wedding the city council
treatment, beginning with how the groom's mother made
a pass at him by the reception table.

10

A GORGEOUS MAN and a gorgeous day. Even if she was on a mission, Lissa wasn't going to let those elements go to waste. She'd filled Mick's cooler with a few bottles of white wine, a brick of cheese and some grapes. Who knew that Mick, whose idea of a great lunch was a greasy steak in a sack, sported such gems in his refrigerator? Lissa sat back in her chair and sighed in contentment.

"What are you so happy about?" Scott asked. He'd been in a touchy mood ever since she refused to help him start the boat. Lissa firmly believed there were things that every man should know how to do: driving a stick-shift vehicle, mowing the grass and killing spiders were a few of them. Starting boats had just been added to that category. After flooding the engine once, they were finally tooling down the lake.

"So I've never gotten a chance to ask you how your career as a novelist is going," Lissa said.

He slumped back in the captain's seat. "If you're trying to cheer me up, that's not the way to do it."

"Your novels are still unpublished, huh?"

"Mostly they're still unwritten."

"You know, if I were you, I'd write a book about what kind of person Miranda really is. You could sell it for scads of money." Lissa was a firm believer in working with the assets you had at hand.

"Nah. I couldn't sell out my art like that."

She leaned back in her chair. "Well, how do you support yourself?"

"I have a trust fund, for one thing."

"You do?" Lissa's heart soared. Why had Claire never mentioned this to her?

"But it only pays five hundred dollars a month," he said. "So I temp the rest of the time."

"Five hundred dollars? Temp?" She felt like she was back in freshmen economics, so convoluted were the principles he was trying to explain to her. "I never heard of a trust fund that didn't support its recipient. What kind of trust fund is that?"

"The kind I have, with my kind of luck."

At that, the motor made kind of a weird lurching sound, then all was still.

They looked at each other. Scott's mood had been so fragile, she was almost afraid to speak. "What now?" Lissa asked.

Scott shrugged. "Break out the wine, I guess. It's been that kind of day."

HER STORY WAS FINISHED. Gathering up the pieces of stationery she'd used, Claire couldn't help admiring her work. She'd chronicled, logically and thoroughly, how, since 1970, Carbine Industries had begun dumping toxic wastes on properties in south Ridgeville. She'd put in the "no comments" from the plant's officials, the angry testimony of the residents there, and she unraveled, as best she could, the tangled question of who owned the properties. In her heart, she knew it was a solid piece of reporting. But would it ever see print?

That was up to Alec, she knew. His laptop and modem were sitting on the desk. Just as soon as he'd written his profile of Miranda, he'd zap it in over the phone line and see it become front-page material in next week's edition.

And what would she have in that issue? A puff piece on a local author, a few movie reviews...

Oh, no. She hadn't put any of that stuff on the paper's computer drive before she left. It was all sitting on a diskette next to her own computer. Glancing at her watch, she took a chance that Allie would be home. She grabbed the phone and called her.

"Allie, I need you to do a huge favor for me."

"Have you slept with him yet?"

"What kind of question is that?" Claire asked.

"That sounds to me like you think you're very close. Just remember, it's like driving, something you never forget." Allie paused, then said, "I forgot what a terrible driver you are. It's just a figure of speech."

"Get this straight. I am not sleeping with Alec Mason."

"Do you really want Scott Granville to be it? Do you want to go to your grave knowing that sleazy, low-life little cheater was the last man to make love to you?"

"Thanks for your concern, but I'm sure I'll have plenty of opportunities to sleep around before I die," she told Allie. "You, though, are in imminent danger of losing your life unless you shut up and listen to me."

"All right," Allie said. "What do you need me to do?"

Claire explained about the diskette.

"I'd wait until we got back, but the production staff was going to lay out the life-style section this weekend. Just go slip it under the door to the newspaper office. I don't think anyone will be there."

"That's comforting to know, considering I'll be walking around downtown all by myself."

"Oh, don't worry about that," Claire said. "There's a regular group of bums who hang out in front of the building. They watch out for guys who try to harass women."

"How comforting," Allie said. "I guess the key's in the bird feeder where it always is?"

"Yes," Claire said. "I really appreciate this."

"No problem," Allie said. "And, Claire? Don't forget to use protection. Remember, I . . ."

Blushing, Claire hung up on Allie and sat on the bed for a second before leaning back into it. She wrapped last night's blanket around her and imagined that she could still smell Alec's scent in it. Here the two of them had lain together all night, with Claire blissfully unaware of whatever it was that was protecting her from unpleasant dreams. What if she had known? Could she have stopped herself from sliding her hand under his shirt and feeling his powerful chest muscles? What would she have done if she had felt his hands caressing her thighs, if she had felt his mouth warm and hungry on her neck?

She sighed and rolled herself up more tightly in the blanket, unable to stop herself from fantasizing about Alec's hands on her. Alec cradling her breast, Alec bringing his delicious lips to hers.

A knock at the door startled her, and she bounded up from the bed. "Just a second," she said, thinking, and hoping, that it was Alec. She prayed that her flushed face wouldn't belie her racy daydreams.

"Chris," she said, opening the door to Miranda's cousin. "What's up?"

"Don't bother to hide your disappointment. That glow in your cheeks gives it all away," he told her. "Your friend Roger sent me to tell you he's getting together a bunch of people to play badminton."

"Badminton?" she echoed.

"And the beautiful redhead at the end of the hall says, 'Not in this lifetime,' " Chris said.

"You know how I am about organized sports," she said.

"I'll break it to Roger gently. I think he thinks you're the outdoor type," Chris said, starting to walk away.

"Hey, Chris," she said, calling him back. "You haven't seen Alec, have you?"

His guilty expression told her he knew something. "Christine caught up with him and Miranda by the pier, and she said Miranda was finally giving Alec that interview he's been hounding her about."

"That's really nice for Alec," Claire said.

"It's your paper, too," Chris reminded her.

"You're right," she told him. "I'm not losing a fiancé, I'm gaining an exclusive." As she was saying it, it didn't even occur to her to confess to Chris that Alec wasn't really her fiancé. The pain was just as real as if he had been.

"Claire." Chris seemed shocked by her cynicism. "It's not like you to be this way."

"But maybe it's about time," she added quietly. He started to walk away again, and she stopped him once more. "I've got to ask you something," she said in a low voice. "Is anyone else around?"

"They're all out in the clean, fresh air."

"Be honest with me. Does your tabloid editor want you to get something from this weekend?"

"I'm sending him something, yes," Chris admitted. "Right now it's going to be as big of a yawn as Miranda's next movie."

"Well, if you found out something about Miranda that you didn't know about, wouldn't you feel obligated to tell him?"

"What are you getting at?" Chris asked. "Do you have something on her?"

Before he had a chance to question her further, she heard Alec whistling as he came down the stairs.

"We'll talk later," she said. Chris nodded and nearly bumped into Alec as he went back up the steps.

"Badminton?" he asked a startled Alec.

"No thanks," Alec said. He stopped at the doorway and gave Claire a hug. She stayed still as a statue at his touch, and she refused to move when he tried to squeeze past her in the doorway.

"Are you going to let me in?" he asked.

"I suppose I must," she said, moving abruptly out of the entrance. He stumbled a little, then shut the door behind him. "I guess it's your room, too."

The room hadn't seemed so small before, not even when she'd woken up to find herself practically on top of him. Alec said nothing, merely leaned against the door and folded his arms, his eyes measuring her with a look she couldn't read. She walked to the desk and straightened the pile of papers there. Then she went to the sofa and pretended to fiddle with something in one of her suitcases. All the time, she could feel Alec's eyes on her.

"Don't you have somewhere else to be?" she asked.

"Like where?"

"Don't you want to go chase Miranda some more?"

"Why should I? I got my story," he said.

"So I heard." Claire popped open another suitcase and began to aimlessly transfer items from one piece of luggage to another. "It's funny, considering that she never meant to go down to the pond to talk to you. I overheard her tell someone she sent you there to get her out of her hair. But when she saw me eating lunch with Roger, she must have wanted to make me jealous." And it worked, she added silently. Her body tensed as she felt Alec step away from the door and come up behind her.

"What were you doing having lunch with Roger?" he asked.

She turned to face him, only to find he was even closer than she thought. She tried to step back, but the sofa was in the way. Lifting her chin a bit, she said, "What makes it your business?"

"This makes it my business." He put his hand under her chin and pulled her lips to his. It was a sweet kiss, a gentle kiss, and Claire knew she could break away from it, could go on pretending there was nothing between the two of them but a light hint of flirtation. But there was no denying the passion, a passion that made her whole body quake as Alec began to explore her mouth with his tongue, claiming not only her lips but all of her.

She bit his lip, and his arms tightened around her. When one hand moved from around her waist to cup her breast gently, her knees started shaking, and Alec pulled her on top of him as he sat down on the sofa, pushing her suitcases off onto the floor as he did so. Circling and teasing the nipple of her breast through the linen of the shirt, he whispered, "I need to see more of you."

Any feelings of self-consciousness Claire had ever had around Alec were suspended. For how long, she didn't know, but she wanted to revel in the time while she had it, to let him enjoy her body just as she wanted to enjoy his.

Claire traced her lips down Alec's jaw and neck, bestowing kisses on him as his fingers moved down the buttons of her shirt. He pushed his hands into her blouse, moving his strong, warm fingers to the snap on her bra.

Claire watched, her ache for him almost uncontrollable, as his tongue licked her nipple before he took all of her in his mouth.

Desperate to feel his skin against hers, Claire tugged at his shirt, pulling it out of his jeans and pushing it up, then running her nails along his hard stomach. As she shifted her weight, she felt the hardness of him pulse under her, and she pressed herself against him.

"Oh, Claire," Alec said, letting go her swollen breast to slip his shirt over his head. "You're everything perfect, did you know that?"

In answer, she kissed him, and as their tongues teased one another, Claire felt Alec's hand pop the button on her khakis and ease the zipper down, his fingers brushing against her. Still kissing him, she rose a little, needing for him to be able to touch her. Her own fingers went to the button on his jeans, and she felt the bulge of him just as his fingers slipped under the white cotton of her panties.

Two fingers went inside her, as his thumb found the locus of her desire, and he taunted her with his touch. She rubbed her face against his hair, cradling him against her chest.

She cried out as his hand pulled away from her, but he used both hands to pull her pants off, then stretched her legs out across the couch as he shed his own jeans.

He was standing beside her, wearing only his briefs, and she couldn't stop looking at him, couldn't let go the sight of his muscular body. She reached out and traced her fingers along him, feeling the uneasy heat raging through her own body as she watched him shudder.

"You're so beautiful," she said to him. She took his hands and pulled him down on the couch, loving the feel of his whole body stretched out against hers. His briefs were the only thing keeping them apart, and when she felt the rock-solidness of him move against her, she reached to pull the shorts down.

He moved her hand back up to his stomach, and began caressing her along the length of her inner thighs, making her catch her breath.

"Claire," he whispered. "I don't have anything."

It doesn't matter, she wanted to say. She wanted him inside of her, damn the consequences. She reached to touch him again, then stopped. "A friend . . . um, she gave me something. It might be in my purse."

Alec rolled off her as she lowered herself to the floor and crawled past the suitcases to her purse a couple of feet away. She dug through it frantically, finally spilling the contents as Alec leaned down over her, tracing kisses along her back and moving her legs apart as he touched the inner core of her again.

She had just decided to give herself up to the storm that was brewing inside of her when she saw the red, foil-wrapped condom under a stack of bank receipts.

She handed it to him, and suddenly what hadn't seemed possible was really happening. Within a moment, he was inside her. She gripped his shoulders as he pushed against her.

"My sweet Claire," he said. "You feel so good."

All her words were flying away, replaced only by the powerful sense of being taken somewhere where her language, her gift of words, would not help her. She had only Alec as her guide, only Alec to help her navigate whatever terrain they were entering.

He rolled over, pulling her on top of him, clutching her hips as she felt herself losing control. She, who'd kept her emotions and her body locked up as tightly as possible, now felt her world collapse, crying out at the wave that built and crashed inside of her. She slumped against Alec, his hands pulling her hair, and his lips whispering her name again. He drove into her twice more before he, too, was still.

She blinked against the tears she was threatening to shed, then buried her face in Alec's chest as she felt his arms encircle her and felt the brush of his lips against her hair.

She didn't say anything, just drifted into sleepy daydreams as they curled together on the floor, saying nothing.

"I love you, Claire," she thought she heard him whisper, but by that time she had fallen too far asleep to be able to respond in kind.

HANK HEARD the obnoxious blast of the newsroom phone and reached blindly for it.

"*Weekly Tribune,*" he said, hoping his voice didn't betray his sleepiness.

"Wake up, Rip Van W.," Mick barked. "My damn boat's been stolen."

Hank took a second to process the information. "But you aren't supposed to be on your boat anyway."

"Look. Right in front of you is the disk with my stories." Hank looked. Unbelievable, but it was there. "Now, are you going to help me or not?"

"Let's think this through," Hank said, rubbing his eyes a little. "Is anything else missing?"

"Some stuff out of the fridge, but there's an ugly old Maverick parked in my driveway. There was also a mascara tube in my bathroom." Mick's voice became even more outraged. "There hasn't been mascara in my bathroom since my wife left."

Hank moved to forestall the monologue that went with any mention of Mick's ex-wife, but he was too late.

"She said, I'm not coming back until you learn there's more to life than newspaper stories and fishing rods."

"Now that your boat's been stolen, maybe you won't be fishing as much," Hank said.

"I even stay stocked up on the foods she likes, in case she decides to stop by," Mick continued.

"Have you called the police?" Hank interrupted.

"Not yet," Mick said. "I wanted to call you first, find out if you had any ideas."

Thinking that was one of the most flattering, if not one of the smartest, things he'd heard in a while, Hank was about to answer Mick when the other line rang.

"Just a second," he said. *"Weekly Tribune."*

A country voice answered his hello. "I'm looking for Lissa Barnard."

"She won't be in until Monday," Hank said. If her social calendar permits, he added silently. "I can take a message, though."

"This is Eddie, of Eddie's Garage and Parts Shop," the man said. "I had kind of a slow day over here at the shop, and I was able to get that red baby of hers running again. It's supposed to be the customer's own fault when their car's damaged by towing, but tell her I'm not going to charge her anything. She can just bring my Maverick back.''

"Your Maverick?" Hank asked.

"I don't usually loan cars," Eddie said. "She was with her sister's old boyfriend, though—the one who went to the rain forest—and she was trying to get them back together again."

"She's nice that way," Hank said.

"Maybe if the sister won't take this guy back, the two of them could go out," Eddie said. "They looked cute together."

"Try not to think along those lines, Eddie," Hank said. He thanked him for his call, then clicked back to Mick.

"Did you get dictation straight from Rome or something?" Mick asked.

"I know where your boat is," Hank said. "Do you know how to get to Miranda Craig's house on the lake?"

"I know how to get there by boat."

"You don't have a boat, Mick. By land." Hank paused to let Mick think, and as he did, a movement at the door caught his eye. A floppy disk with a stuck-on label was shoved under the door and onto the carpet. "Hang on," he told Mick and dropped the phone onto the desk. He threw the door open just in time to see a black-haired girl in a short, bouncy skirt and fashionable jacket straighten up from her crouch on the floor. When she saw Hank, she jumped.

"You scared me to death," she said, putting her hand over her heart. "Claire said no one would be here when I came to drop the disk off."

"Claire said..." Hank repeated. "Listen, do you know how to get to Miranda Craig's place on the lake?"

The woman nodded. "Her cousin drove me out there once."

Hank ushered her into the office, to a spot by the door. "Don't move," he said. Picking up the phone again, he said, "Mick, I've got our guide. Her name is um . . ."

"Allie," she supplied.

"Allie," he said into the phone. "We're on our way."

"Let's go," he told Allie, following her out into the hall. He flicked off all but one row of lights, then locked the door behind him. He had taken just a few steps when he stopped and turned back. "Forgot something," he told Allie, unlocking the door and slipping back into the semi-darkened room. He pulled open a drawer at his desk and took an unlabeled floppy out from under some files near the back.

"Now we're ready," he said as he rejoined Allie in the hall. The two of them started on their way.

11

HAD HE EVER TOLD a woman he loved her? His mother, but even that was only on special occasions. That wasn't what he was talking about, though. Had he ever told a *woman* woman?

He hadn't. He'd dated a lot of women, liked some of them an awful lot, but nothing about them had made him want to do anything but run in the other direction the minute he saw they wanted to be something more than good-time girlfriends. If he'd pictured himself voicing the phrase at all, it was to some nameless perfect woman in some incredibly fantastic setting. Instead, he had said it to Claire Morgan, a woman whose flaws he now found irresistible. And they weren't on the top of a skyscraper, fireworks going off around them. They were on the floor of Miranda Craig's guest room. And she hadn't even heard him.

Alec eased himself away from Claire and reached up to the bed for the blanket there. He wrapped it around her, looking at her again as she slept. Gently Alec lifted Claire onto the bed. She stirred a little as he held her, but had soon settled back into sleep. He headed for the shower, and he, who had never had an urge to burst into song in his entire life, had to restrain from humming the whole time he was in there. Being in love was one thing, but turning into a major-class goof was another.

When he emerged from the bathroom, his hair freshly dried, his face clean shaven and his shirt crisp and pressed,

Claire was still asleep. The cold-shower remedy had done nothing for him, and as much as Alec wanted to do nothing more than sit on the bed and stare at Claire, he thought he should probably do something a bit more constructive with his time. Old habits die hard, he told himself.

He knew he couldn't get his Miranda Craig story completely written before dinner, but he could start transcribing their talk, anyway. He flicked on his laptop, rewound the tape and plugged the headphones into the small tape recorder. He'd heard the first notes of Miranda's voice when a guilty feeling made him look back toward Claire. Was he going to look like a jerk if she woke up and found him working? On the other hand, if he did nothing but sit and watch her sleep for the next hour or so, he was really going to look like someone with no inner resources.

Slipping the headphones off, he rubbed his hand through his hair. Never had a woman made him question everything about himself. He couldn't even transfer words from tape onto paper without indulging in some kind of love-stricken existential crisis. He rewound the tape to the very beginning again, put the headphones on and steeled himself to get to work. Force of habit made him crave a cola or coffee while he typed, and he leaned over to the minirefrigerator to see if there were any colas there.

He pushed a bottle of Chardonnay out of the way to grab a diet cola, then snatched up the bottle, too, in case Claire wanted to have some when she woke up. There were some cut-up and covered chunks of cheese on the bottom shelf, as well as some chocolate confections that looked suspiciously like truffles. Alec added all this to his haul, then got up to move the stuff to the small table on the other side of the room. As he stood, his hip knocked off Claire's collection of papers. Bending down to retrieve them, he remembered she said she was going to work on the south Ridgeville story.

He looked at the first paragraph. "Terri McCormick used to play tag in the high grasses of the field next door to her house. She and her friends would chase each other, shrieking and squealing, until they fell exhausted onto the bumpy ground. They would lie there in giggling heaps, quieting only to listen for their mothers calling them to supper or to pay silent childish homage to the awesome sunsets in the sky far above them. McCormick, who is raising her own daughter in the same neighborhood, wishes her daughter could run, carefree, in that field. But she says for more than two decades harmful toxins have been dumped there, mostly under the cover of darkness, rendering that land and two other Ridgeville sites dangerously polluted, if not deadly."

Not bad, Alec thought to himself. A little prosy, maybe, but that could be cleaned up. He read the next paragraph, then sat down and slipped off the headphones. He read to the end and began the story again, the wine and cola warming unopened, the truffles and cheese still sitting covered on the desk.

CLAIRE ALWAYS HAD incredibly vivid dreams, but this one had been something else all together. She and Alec had been together on the floor of the guest room, having the best sex she'd ever had in her whole life. The way her body felt even now, so well loved. She didn't know you could dream physical sensations so accurately.

Claire stretched a little, still mostly asleep, and pulled the covers around her. She snuggled tighter against the blanket, warm and scratchy against her bare skin.

Her bare skin? *Now* she was awake. Claire sat up in bed, her heart racing, and peeked at herself under the blanket. Yes, she was completely naked. She looked around for Alec, then saw him, dressed for dinner and sitting at the desk with his back to her. If her nearsighted eyes weren't deceiving her, he was looking at the pink pages of her story as he typed on his laptop.

It was all too much. Claire sunk back into the bed, closing her eyes and feigning sleep again so she could dwell on what had happened in this room between the two of them. The way he had touched her, the way his mouth had traveled along her breasts, the sweet things he'd whispered to her. If she'd thought for a second that those were the fantasies of an overheated mind, waking up naked was all the evidence she needed that their lovemaking had been real indeed. And had she heard him say he loved her as she drifted to sleep? Or had that part of it been a dream?

Sitting up again, she saw that Alec was still absorbed in whatever he was doing. Clutching the blanket to her, she reached down from the bed and silently dragged one of her suitcases across the carpet. Her eyes strayed to her "comfort clothes"—bicycle shorts and a wildlife T-shirt in XL. She knew she should be trying to impress Alec with her new wardrobe, but after the tumultuous events of the day, she had a craving to be plain old Claire for a few minutes. She could at least wear this until it was time for dinner.

She dressed in bed, and although she made as little noise as possible, she thought it was strange that Alec was so completely engrossed in what he was doing that he didn't seem to sense any stirring in the room at all. Not sure what to say to him, she settled for clearing her throat as she walked across the room. He didn't hear her. She tried again, just two feet away from him, but still got no response.

"Alec," she said firmly. Expecting him to be startled, she saw he was so into whatever it was he was doing that the sound of her voice didn't even phase him.

He looked up at her and smiled, typing a few words even as he did so. "Did you sleep well?" he asked, turning back to the page. "You look great."

"I don't think you looked at me," she said.

"Short tight black pants, shirt with some kind of endangered species you probably think we should save," he said, his eyes still on the text and his fingers still moving across the keyboard. "Hang on till I get to a stopping place." He went for another thirty seconds, then quit. Half standing up, he leaned over and gave Claire a full kiss on the mouth, then sat back down again and resumed work.

I'd better sit down, too, she thought. As Alec typed, she tried to sum up what seemed to be a truly bizarre situation. Alec appeared to be putting the manuscript of her story into his laptop. Shoved to one side of the desk was a collection of cheese, chocolate, cola and wine, all of it unopened.

"Are you about to have some kind of feast?" she asked him.

He looked up again. "Oh. You mean all this stuff? I got it out, but then I got sidetracked. Have some."

"Thanks." She got a couple of wineglasses down from the small cabinet over the refrigerator and found a corkscrew there, too. "Would you like to do the honors?"

"What? The corkscrew? Oh, sure. Just a sec." He reached another stopping place, then quickly uncorked the wine and handed it back to her. "Do you mind pouring? I want to get as much of this in as possible before dinner."

Claire spoke slowly, trying to figure it all out as she talked. "As much of my story put into the computer as possible. Because... because why?"

Alec held his finger on the page to mark where he'd quit. "It's running next week, in the slot I had for the Miranda interview. That means it's got to go to production by Monday. I don't think it needs much work, though."

"You don't think it needs much work? To run in next week's issue?"

He pointed at her with the finger that wasn't marking his place. "I like how it isn't all Harlan Edwards. But one thing I think you need to do is make it more obvious that this corporation guy, Blalock, knows what's going on and is just stonewalling you and everyone else."

He sounded serious. He didn't sound like he'd agreed to consider running her story, but like he was really burning the late-afternoon oil to get it into shape. This was more than odd. This was fishy.

"Alec," she said. "I know why you're doing this, and you don't have to."

"Doing what? Putting your story in this week's paper? If you think I'm just doing it because I'm in love with you, that's not it."

"Oh." That hadn't been what she was thinking, but hearing him deny it was pretty crushing anyway. "No, what I meant was..."

Sneaking in a few words as they spoke, Alec continued, "I'd be doing it even if I wasn't in love with you. It's a great story."

Claire sneaked a longing glance at Alec's tape recorder. If her horse and carriage turned into a pumpkin after she left here, she'd at least like to have some proof that those two remarkable phrases had come out of Alec's mouth. "What did you say?"

"I'm in love with you. This is a great story." He grinned at her wickedly. "Which part sounds too good to be true?"

Both, she thought to herself, but she said, "Alec, you think that if you act enthusiastic about this, I won't judge you for your story on Miranda. I don't anyway. Go ahead and write your interview with Miranda. I know it's going to move a lot of copies."

"Damn right it will," Alec said, turning back to her story. "It's going to be a really hot story. I got great quotes from her."

Claire remembered her earlier conversation with Chris. "Listen, did you..."

He continued talking, "But you've got this quote from Senator Johnson in here, back when he promised to something about the dumping. He's going to be in town on Thursday, so maybe we can get some publicity for the paper if we tie that in with his visit. The Miranda thing is an evergreen, something that won't date if it isn't published right away." Rifling through the pink papers, he turned to her and said, "Pictures."

It took her a second to hop on board his train of thought. "You mean do I have any? A few."

"Well, we can always cut out of here early tomorrow and go up to the sites."

Claire knew she was hearing more than she deserved to hear. Looking this particular gift horse in the ivories was a bad idea, but she couldn't help herself. "Well, maybe you could run them both."

"Two big scoops in one week and nothing in the next?" He shook his head. "We want to give readers the impression that this isn't a fluke, that we're going to come up with great stuff every week."

Thinking she'd wait until later to remind him that he hadn't previously given two shakes about those readers, Claire said, "You see, I was kind of hinting to Chris that I was going to tell Christine something no one else knew about Miranda." She took a truffle from the plate. "By the way, how did that part of the interview go? I expect she denied it, but that's okay. I mean, Trent Daniels will certainly back us up."

"Give me five seconds, and I'll be done with this. I'm a crackerjack two-fingered typist."

Claire waited, watching him type his story. "That got it." He turned and took a chunk of cheese from the plate. "Can I have a sip of your wine?"

She gave him a sip, and he said, "Now what were you saying about Chris? Was it about him asking me to play badminton on the stairs a while ago?"

"Not exactly," Claire said. "I let him think I was going to say something big about Miranda tonight during the interview. Now, I'm not stupid. I know it will get cut out. But if Chris is in the room, he can report the story anyway. 'Secret revelations about ruthless screen heroine.' Something like that. But if you wait to print your story, it means you'll get scooped by the tabloids.''

Alec's face held a troubled look, one she couldn't read. "First of all, I don't consider those papers my competition.''

Claire stared at him. "You mean you don't care if they get the story first?''

"I'm not doing that kind of story. I'm doing an in-depth profile of a local actress. It won't include any mention of what you told me.''

She couldn't believe what she was hearing. "Now whose horse is wearing platform shoes?''

Alec busied himself with configuring his modem and dialing into the paper. "You asked me not to mention it.''

"I changed my mind,'' she said.

"So did I,'' he told her. The silence that followed was broken by the sound of the modem dialing and connecting.

"Tell me why,'' Claire said, not sure she wanted to hear the answer. "Did she sweet-talk you out of mentioning it? Did she whisper in your ear that little old her would just be devastated if people thought she was anything less than a paragon of virtue? You said yourself it was just a college play.'' She hated what she heard herself say next. "How many kisses did it take to change your mind?''

"I can't believe you would say that after what just happened here,'' Alec said, standing to face her. "I felt sorry for her, okay?''

"Sorry? Sorry that last month she was on the cover of two magazines rather than five?''

"She might have gone out there to make you jealous. She might have even considered making a play for me. But she didn't. Once she realized that my mind was on you and nobody but you, she considered me a sympathetic ear. She let her guard down around me. There was no spark between us, Claire. I promise you that. And she was honest enough to let me see that she's eaten up with envy over you. Even somebody as emotionally dense as I am can see that's why she made off with Scott.''

Someone keep him away from the self-help books, Claire thought to herself. Pop psychology was not his forte. "Why would she be jealous of me?"

"A thousand reasons. Because she grew up thinking how much prettier and smarter you were."

Claire was amazed. "Did she tell you that?"

"Yes, she did," Alec said. "She's also jealous of how talented you are, as a writer and as an actress."

Claire grew suspicious. "You're telling me all this so I'll change my mind about what to tell Christine."

"It's your secret," Alec said. "I can't tell you not to reveal it. If it had been mine, I would have written about it years ago."

"That's the point," Claire said hotly. "I'm tired of forgiving and forgetting. The fact remains, she got mad at me because I had lunch with her boyfriend, and she thought she'd make a play for you in turn."

Alec shrugged. "If that's the way you see it. I see someone who looks in the mirror every day and wishes she were more like you."

There was no use continuing this argument. Claire stood up and got her clothes together, grabbing an elegant black jumpsuit out of a suitcase. She was going to be on her best behavior at the dinner table, she decided, but that didn't mean she had to fade into the mashed potatoes. Playing at self-confidence this weekend was leading her to believe it wouldn't be such a bad thing if that character were a regular part of her life.

"I'm going to get ready," Claire said.

Alec shut off his computer. "Do what you have to do."

I will, Claire thought to herself. I will.

HANK EXPECTED MICK TO BE at the front door, hat on, ready to go. Instead, he greeted them with a leisurely "Come in, come in. Come have a drink.

You won't believe who stopped by," Mick said, pointing to a plump, pretty woman in her fifties who was seated at the kitchen table.

"The former Mrs. Regan?" Hank guessed.

"That's her," Mick said, beaming. "She came to talk to me about our daughter Sally. Who's this?"

Hank introduced Allie, reminding him that she knew how to get to Miranda's.

Mick took another sip of his bourbon. "You know, I'm not in any hurry to get the boat back this evening. It can wait."

"Oh." Hank and Allie said with one voice. Hank took the unlabeled computer diskette out of his pocket and turned it over in his hands before putting it back. "Okay, then," he said. "I guess we'll head back into town."

"Sure," Allie said.

Mrs. Regan looked from one face to the other. "You know, Mick," she said. "I think I'd like to go with them. I've heard the house is gorgeous, and it isn't often I get to peek into the life of a real Hollywood star."

Hank, who knew from Mick's tirades that the former Mrs. Regan was less impressed by money than almost anyone else, silently thanked her.

Allie took the car keys from Hank's hand and jiggled them. "Let's go, guys. This band of intruders is about to storm Miranda Craig's gate."

12

"DO YOU THINK there's some kind of universal distress signal for SOS?" Lissa was stretched out on the floor of the flat-bottomed boat, watching the sky as the sun crawled to sleep over the horizon.

"You mean besides jumping up and down and waving our arms?" Scott asked. He was lying beside her.

"That didn't work very well for us, did it?" Lissa asked. In between eating cheese, drinking wine and talking, they'd made what they hoped were enthusiastic overtures at everyone who had passed by them. But the other boaters, with their smiles, waves and hoots, apparently thought they were just trying to express their feelings of solidarity and fellowship.

Scott said, "I never had any reason to know them. Signals. It shows how little you ever really know about what's going to happen in your life."

"I know just what you mean," Lissa said, leaning up on one elbow to look at him. "How stuff you thought was important just isn't."

He leaned toward her, and she waited for his kiss. Just then, she heard the unmistakable sounds of an outboard motor.

"Did you hear that?" Scott asked her. She nodded and they stood up, rocking the boat a bit as they waved and hollered at a small army green boat named *Mary Sue*.

Unlike the boaters who had waved back at them, he

hurried over. Cutting off the motor, he said, "I'm Andy Milton. You folks having some kind of trouble?"

Scott explained what the motor was doing, or, more accurately, not doing.

"I'm afraid I'm a fisherman, not a boat mechanic," Andy said, gesturing to the bucket of fish he had in his boat. "If you all want to catch a ride with me to my house, though, you can call somebody about your boat from there. Then I could give you a ride back home."

"Actually," Lissa said, "we were sort of expected at Miranda Craig's. Do you know where that is?"

"Oh, sure. It's about three-quarters of a mile down the road from my house. There's a big to-do going on there this weekend, I heard."

"Yes, there is," Lissa said. "Some friends of ours are there, and they invited us to sail on over this afternoon."

"Just hop on in here, and as soon as we drop these fish off at my place, I'll drive you over there."

With reluctance, Lissa agreed that they should leave their stuff in Mick's boat. Scott helped her into the other, and they were off.

"Sit anywhere you don't see a fish," Andy yelled over the motor.

That was more difficult than it sounded. There were fish, remnants of fish or the definite smell of fish everywhere in the boat. Finally Lissa located a small space on the seat that appeared to be free of any kind of water-life ooze. Scott, who was apparently less picky, plopped down beside her.

She was finally going to get to Miranda Craig's house. She'd get an intimate peek at the life-style of Ridgeville's most celebrated citizen. She'd toss out amusing bons mots to those who would appreciate her for the witty and sophisticated woman she was. And Scott would get to see Claire. Suddenly that didn't sound so appealing.

"So I guess you're really eager to get there, huh?" Lissa said.

"To see Claire? Oh, yeah. That'll be great." The words came out in a total monotone, and Scott rested his chin on his hand and stared at the boat floor. Then he seemed to brighten a little, and he looked up at her. "Say, you don't think that Claire and this guy she went with . . ."

Lissa sighed. "Not a chance."

After a couple of minutes, Andy pulled up to boat dock in back of rambling, comfortable home. He dumped the fish into an outside cooler, then ushered them into the house, hollering as he walked in, "Company, Mary Sue."

Mary Sue was a trim, twinkly version of Andy himself. They introduced themselves, but Lissa found it hard to keep her mind on the introductions with the comforting, peppery aroma of fried chicken wafting through the air. Having eaten only cheese and grapes all day, Lissa forgot all about her recent conversion to vegetarianism as her stomach gave an audible growl. Scott's stomach echoed the cry.

"You kids are starving," Mary Sue said. "Stay for dinner."

"I told them I'd give them a run out to the Craigs' house," Andy told his wife. "They're going to a party there."

Mary Sue put her hands on her hips. "Not without eating something first they aren't."

"Oh, no, Mrs. Milton. We couldn't possibly," Lissa said. She tried to make herself sound convincing. Had they gone all this way and struggled so hard just to give it all up for a home-cooked meal? Besides, she reminded herself, she owed it to Claire to see whether there was anything left between her and her old boyfriend. She hadn't dragged him down from New York City just so she herself could have her way with him.

"Come look at what all I've cooked," Mary Sue said, motioning them to follow her into the large kitchen. There on the countertop was fried chicken, plus a serving bowl full of creamy mashed potatoes and a platter of flaky oversize biscuits. A pecan pie sat next to the biscuits. Lissa felt Scott tremble a little beside her.

"You've got to stay and help us eat some of this food. I always forget I'm cooking for just the two of us, and most of it will wind up going to the cats." She got some plates down from the cabinet. "We wouldn't be eating so late, except that Andy's been out on the boat all day. I know dinner's over for the Craigs. You won't be getting a thing to eat."

"Nothing to eat," Scott echoed.

"Oh, I'm sure they'll dig up some hors d'oeuvres," Lissa said, taking Scott by the elbow and digging her nails into him slightly.

Mary Sue sighed and looked away from them, looking as disappointed as Lissa's kindergarten teacher had once been when she refused to join the clean plate club. She folded her arms across her chest. "Andy, I won't let you drive them down the road until they've had a decent meal."

"Oh, no, we can't," Lissa said.

"Why don't you put a little something away first, then head down there?" the woman asked.

"Yeah," Scott said. "Why don't we put a little something away first, then head down there?"

Lissa narrowed her eyes at him while keeping an apparent smile on her face for the benefit of the Miltons. "Maybe you're right," she said sweetly. "It's very kind of you to think about us. Is there a place where we could freshen up for dinner?"

She and Scott were directed toward the bathroom at the end of the hall, and they shambled off toward it.

"After you," Scott said.

Lissa motioned for him to be quiet, and pulled open a couple of doors near the bathroom till she found one that opened onto a flight of stairs. She motioned for him to follow her as she crept down the stairs and out of the basement through a side door.

"We'll walk there. Miranda's house is just three-quarters of a mile down the road that way," she said, pointing to her right.

Scott frowned. "No, it's three-quarters of a mile down the road that way," he said, pointing left. "Listen, since we're not sure, let's go in there and eat some fried chicken and wait on Mr. Milton."

Lissa shook her head furiously. "Did you see how slowly everything moves in there? We'd still be on dessert and coffee when everyone was packing up and going back to California." Poor thing—he did look hungry, and she patted him on the shoulder for encouragement. "I'm sure they'll be heavy hors d'oeuvres." She started up the driveway, Scott behind her, and he followed her without comment as they turned right up the road.

Forty minutes later, they had seen nothing resembling Miranda Craig's home. They looked at each other, then turned and walked left, trudging onward past the Miltons' inviting home. Evening turned to night as they kept up a pace that would have been the envy of any power walker in the mall, but the road only seemed to get longer and more uninhabited the farther they walked.

"Do you see any signs of life?" Scott asked.

"As a matter of fact, I do. A wall." As they walked toward the entrance, a collection of voices carried to them. Lissa thought them disturbingly familiar voices. She ducked down, and motioned for Scott to follow. Lissa crept along the wall until she came to a place where she could see. She looked, then looked again. It seemed to be Mick and Hank, with two strange women, all of them standing outside of Hank's car and arguing with a man in a security guard's uniform.

"I'm telling you, there's an emergency on the paper he's got to know about," she heard Hank yell.

"Who are those guys?" Scott whispered.

"Not my fan club, that's for sure," Lissa said back. "It doesn't look like he's going to let them in."

She crept a little closer to get a better angle on the situation. Everyone was out of the car, Mick and Hank and a cute girl in a short skirt gesturing wildly, an older woman hanging back with a smile on her face. The security guard was standing in front of them, shaking his head no. The gate behind him was shut tight.

She gestured to Scott, and he crouched down beside her. "Here's what we can do," she whispered. "We can go plead our case with Dudley Doright. Or we can go over the wall."

He looked up at the wall, then at the tree next to it.

"I'll lift you over, then I'll climb up this tree and hop over that way. Are you ready?" he asked her.

"Ready," she said, putting her foot in his hand. "Do you know what, Scott?" she whispered before he lifted her up. "As much as I never really wanted to be one, this makes me feel like a real reporter."

"GOT IT," the hairdresser said, snagging the last tangle out of Claire's hair.

"Ouch," she said, and thought she saw Miranda smirk a little beside her.

"Thick hair tangles up for no reason," the hairdresser said sympathetically. "If you don't want tangles, you should have hair like Miranda's. It's so thin that it's barely there."

"Could we get these people off the set please?" Miranda yelled, swatting away the makeup artist who'd bent down to give her one more look.

"'Touchy,''' the hairdresser muttered as she walked away.

They were seated in the summer den, finally ready to do the joint interview Miranda had promised Christine. Although Miranda had greeted Alec warmly at dinner, she'd been edgy and short with Claire. Fortunately, they hadn't had to sit at her table, although that didn't ease the tension between Alec and Claire. He said Miranda's foul mood was because she was finally facing her envy of Claire. Claire thought it was because she sensed that the new, assertive Claire wasn't going to let her get away with trying to steal another fiancé, even a fake one.

Christine signaled for silence, and those gathered to watch the taping quickly quieted. Chris was there, looking eager and impatient. Larry and Roger were standing along one wall, Alec near them.

Christine began. "Most little girls have best friends, but for many of them that lineup changes from time to time. You two were always inseparable. Miranda, can you tell us what made you want to be Claire's friend?"

"She was smart," Miranda said, with a glance toward Claire that Claire read as, *See, aren't I being nice to you?* Miranda continued, "She was pretty. And she always listened to me."

"Did everything you told me to do," Claire filled in.

"That's right," Miranda said, then realized what she'd agreed to. "Oh, you know, I might have been sort of bossy, the way little girls are."

Claire nodded her agreement. Christine's eyebrows knitted together in a frown, and she looked at her notes.

"Tell me, was there ever any competition between the two of you?"

"Not really," Claire said, figuring she could play straight person for at least one or two questions. "I was into books, and she was into sports, so we were never competitive that way."

"And then, I'm not competitive anyway. I'm one of those people who does best in harmonious, cooperative situations," Miranda added.

That didn't even come from Miranda's head, Claire thought. "I'm afraid she's playing down some essential parts of her personality," she said. "Miranda is one of the most competitive people I know."

"How so?" Christine asked.

How could she resist an opening like this? "Once when we were playing Monopoly, she hit me over the head when I got Park Place. She got to be Donald Trump that day, that's for sure." She turned to watch Miranda's expression. "And then there was a play, in college, and Miranda really wanted the role. She wanted it so badly that she..." Her former friend's face turned ashen, and she gaped for air like a fish. Claire felt a tinge of triumph before she looked across at Alec. He turned away, plainly disgusted by what she was about to do. Didn't he understand that this was her only means of getting back at Miranda? Back at her for what? She could practically hear his voice in her head. For flirting with him because she felt insecure? For constantly trying to prove that she was better than Claire? That wasn't something to get back at someone for; that was something that should inspire pity and compassion.

"She wanted it so badly that?" Christine prompted.

"Oh," Claire said, coming out of her reverie. She looked into Miranda's eyes and said, "That she was devastated when she actually played the role, and I wound up getting a better review for the part she'd abandoned."

"I see." Christine went on to another question, and Miranda's eyes offered up silent gratitude to Claire. She looked at Alec, who smiled back.

"So were you two ever competitive over stage roles?" Christine asked.

"No," Claire said. "I didn't act in college, except for that once. And before that, I never tried to compete with her for the roles she wanted. It just wasn't that important to me.'' As she said it, she realized she was saying it not because she was trying to be self-serving, but because she now knew that had been a key issue of her friendship with Miranda. She hadn't wanted to undermine Miranda's confidence on things that were important to her. She had cared about Miranda's feelings enough to watch what she said and did around her. If Miranda had never learned those particular lessons of friendship, she had still been an important part of Claire's life.

She mulled all this over, continuing to lob back easy answers to Christine's questions, joining in with Miranda where it seemed appropriate. Miranda made a sign with her hands and said, ''Can we take a break?''

''Cut,'' someone yelled as Miranda got up and stretched. ''I'm going to get a cola.'' She turned to Claire. ''Do you want one?''

''I'd like that, thanks,'' Claire said, knowing how difficult it was for the other woman to put herself out after getting used to having her own whims catered to every second of the day. It was just a soda, but it was a start.

As she walked out of the room, almost everyone there, with the exception of Alec, offered to retrieve the soda for her, but she waved them away. ''I need a walk,'' she said.

Claire stayed where she was, eyeing Alec on his side of the room. When Christine stepped away from the camera, Alec came over and sat beside her, taking her hand in his.

''You're holding my hand?'' she asked. ''Come on, for what I did, I deserve better than that.''

''How about this?'' He kissed her then, and all the sounds and distractions in the room faded. She broke off the kiss to look at him, brushing a curly lock away from his forehead.

''I didn't just do it because you wanted me to,'' she said.

"Believe me, I know," Alec told her. "I don't expect that at any time during our lives together you're going to do something just because I want you to."

"During our lives together?" Claire asked. "Don't you mean during our phony engagement?"

He tapped the sapphire ring. "About that phony engagement. Let's make it real."

"How? By blowing on the stone and saying Abracadabra?"

"No. By swearing to love each other for the rest of our lives," he said, holding her close.

"Alec, I swear."

It was a wonderful moment, one she would have liked to have savored, but it was interrupted by Miranda's indignant voice saying, "Will you look at what I found in the hallway?" and by a flat, emotionless voice, saying "Claire."

She looked up to see Miranda in front of her, cola apparently forgotten, throwing her hands around and looking like she was on the verge of a hysterical fit. There, beside Miranda, as though he'd materialized in the many times she'd seen him that way in her dreams, stood Scott Granville. There was no leap of emotions on seeing him, no pains in her heart. Face-to-face with him again, she couldn't imagine why she'd spent so many years making herself miserable because of him.

It appeared that Miranda wasn't going to take charge of the situation, and Claire didn't want to. Instead, she said, "Hello, Scott. I'd like you to meet my fiancé, Alec Mason."

Alec stood and shook hands as though meeting her and Miranda's mutual ex-love in Miranda's house was the most natural thing in the world. "What brings you out this way, Scott?"

"I just wanted to say. Um, Claire... I, uh, just came to tell you guys hey."

"Guess what, Claire?" Miranda finally had her voice again. "Scott says hey."

"How sweet," Claire said, pulling Alec down beside her once again.

Frightened, no doubt, by the murderous look on Miranda's face, Scott began backing away from them. A familiar hand shot out of the crowd and held him still, the well-cared for pink nails pinning him in place.

"Claire," Lissa said, emerging from behind Scott. "Don't be mad at Scott. He just wanted to tie up some loose ends with you two, and he thought this would be the best place to do it. He's impetuous, you know."

Claire had to hide her grin. "I don't think I knew that about Scott."

Lissa greeted Alec, then extended a hand to Miranda, "I don't think we've met. I'm Lissa Barnard, the society editor for the *Tribune*."

Miranda grudgingly accepted the handshake, then turned to Claire. "Did you bring the whole staff here or what?"

"No," Claire said, but then heard a noisy argument traveling down the hall toward them. She thought the voices belonged to Hank and Mick. Her suspicions were confirmed when she saw the men enter the room, followed by Allie and an unfamiliar middle-aged woman.

"At least the production and business people aren't here," she told Miranda. "That's a real unstable bunch."

The security guard was close behind them. "They say they had some emergency at the paper, and they've all got to be here to see somebody named Claire and Alec."

Alec stood and turned to Lissa. "Is that how you got in, too?"

Lissa pointed to the tear in her blouse. "We got in the old-fashioned way."

"Ms. Craig, I don't know what to think," the guard told Miranda.

She sighed. "Let them stay."

"But I don't think they had the proper authorization to get in here."

Miranda put her forehead in her hands. "Let them stay. Chris, honey, will you and Larry go round up all the liquor in the house and bring it up here?"

"What's that line from one of those plays you loved?" Claire asked Miranda, knowing she would know what she was talking about.

She smiled. "I'm just having a real bad day," she quoted. She leaned toward Claire and whispered, "I owe you one."

"Forget it," Claire said.

She felt Alec's hand squeeze hers just as she heard Mick's booming voice.

"I think we'd better go hunt for some food," Lissa said, grabbing Scott and slipping into the crowd.

"Don't think I'm not going to ask you where my boat is," Mick called after her. He introduced his ex-wife to Claire and Alec, and Claire introduced the two of them to Miranda.

"Did you have trouble finding the place?" Miranda asked politely.

"Oh, no," Mick said. "Claire's friend Allie found it with no trouble at all."

"I'll bet," Miranda said, as they all looked over to where Allie was drinking wine with Chris and Roger in the corner.

"What was the emergency on the paper?" Claire asked.

"Somehow," Mick said, blushing, "all the stories got thrown away."

Claire and Alec gasped as Mick said. "Hank fixed it, though. He recreated Alec's and Lissa's stories, and Allie dropped off some of Claire's."

Claire looked at Mick, confused. "But if Hank fixed it, why did you all rush out here?"

"Because Scott and Lissa stole my boat," Mick said, as if it were the most obvious thing in the world.

"What?"

Alec bent down to kiss Claire. "I don't understand it, either. Let's agree to figure it out together later."

As she and Alec concluded their kiss, Claire noticed that Miranda was still standing near them, out of the limelight. Claire started to say something to cheer her, but was interrupted by the appearance of Hank. She presented Miranda to Hank, then was as shocked as everyone else apparently was to hear him say to Miranda, "I love your work."

"You do?" Claire felt a teeny stab of guilt when she heard the doubt in Miranda's voice. Surely she hadn't sapped Miranda of her self-esteem forever.

"I really love your part in *Sundays at the Park*. It isn't everyone who can bring that kind of depth to the small role of teen-aged babysitter."

"But you think I did?" Her voice was hopeful.

"Oh, absolutely," he said. "Tell me something I've always wanted to know. In the Rand Walsh art movie *Mystery Generation*, are you the voice of the ex-girlfriend who keeps calling the hero?"

Claire hit herself on the head. "How could I not have known that? I knew that voice was familiar."

Miranda was visibly excited over Hank's discovery. "No one has ever figured that out."

"That voice steals the movie," Hank said. "Why isn't it listed on your résumé?"

Miranda looked a bit downcast. "They didn't list me in the credits because it was such a nonpart, Walsh thought, and I was a nobody. Now he doesn't want to admit that somebody as mainstream as I am was in one of his movies."

Hank shook his head. "He's only shooting himself in the foot with that kind of reverse snobbism."

"Since when do you know about movies?" Alec asked.

Hank kept talking to Miranda. "I think you have the kind of crossover appeal that could bring mainstream audiences to smaller films. I think you especially have a gift for making what may seem to be a small character larger than life. Although I'm sure it will be an excellent movie, *A Woman's Heart* is just that kind of saintly-woman-of-the-South stuff you keep getting handed."

By this time, everyone in the room was openly listening to Hank and Miranda.

"Oh, I know," Miranda said. "I wish someone would give me a script where I played a real person. A working girl, you know, but a funny one. But I don't want there to only be comedy in the script."

"I have a script just like that," Hank said. "One that I wrote especially with you in mind."

As those who knew Hank stood there in stunned silence, Miranda put her hands on her hips, now openly flirting with him. "Do you know how many guys say that to me?"

Hank drew a computer diskette out of his pocket. "But how many of them actually have great scripts? Can we use your computer, Alec?"

"Be my guest."

As the two of them walked off, Mick turned to Claire and Alec and said, "Looks like you two are getting pretty serious about this phony engagement thing."

Miranda stopped and turned around. "Phony engagement?"

Alec waved a hand at her. "Pay no attention to that man behind the curtain."

Claire turned to Alec. "Sweetheart, you made a *Wizard of Oz* reference. Now I know you love me."

Mick and his ex-wife wandered discreetly away. As Claire and Alec started to kiss, they were interrupted by an annoyed Chris. "What about the scoop you were going to reveal?"

"False lead," she said. At his irritated glance, she told him, "But I've got something better. Why don't you phone the tabloid editor and tell him that the script Miranda is looking at is going to be her hottest movie yet? Everyone is going to be talking about Hank Jensen."

"Do you really think so?" Chris asked, scurrying away.

"Alone at last," Claire said, snuggling up to Alec in the crowded room.

"Never alone again," Alec answered her. "Not when we have each other.

They kissed again as Claire heard Lissa say, "Mick, did I ever tell you about my little sister? She'd love to be a society reporter."

Claire and Alec broke off their kiss and smiled at each other. "I forgot to tell you. The psychic also said I was going to have four children and many more grandchildren. Won't this be something to tell them about?"

She looked around the room, where Allie and Roger were laughing in the corner, Renee, Christine and Larry were sharing a bottle of bourbon, Mick and his ex-wife had their arms around each other and Scott was holding hands with Lissa.

"You'd better grab Christine's video recorder," Claire told Alec. "Otherwise, I don't think they're going to believe it."

Epilogue

From the Tribune ...

Morgan-Mason Wedding Bells Chime
by Krista Barnard

Claire Morgan, senior editor of this paper, whose story on toxic dumping in South Ridgeville sparked several criminal and civil investigations and indictments, was wed October 7 to Alec Mason, *Tribune* co-owner and editor in chief. Nuptials were held at the historic Ramsey-Ivy house. The bride's parents were in from Florida for the occasion, and the groom's extended family filled out the crowd.

The bride wore a vintage wedding suit from the 1930s, and her bridesmaid, Allie Reilly of Ridgeville, wore a 1920s flapper dress. Mick Regan, who recently sold part ownership of the paper to Mr. Mason as part of the settlement of libel suits stemming from two of the *Tribune's* stories was the best man.

Among those in attendance were Peggy Regan, former wife of Mr. Regan. Also wishing the bride and groom well were Lissa Barnard, formerly of this newspaper, and her fiancé, Scott Granville, author of the instant bestselling paperback *Bitter Laughter: My Years with Miranda*. Hank Jensen, currently on sabbatical from this paper, sent his regrets from New York City, as did Miranda Craig.

After a brief honeymoon, the couple will reside at the

bride's family home in Ridgeville.

The food was cocatered by Bubba's, this year's winner of the Fourth Annual Roast it Right Barbecue Cook-off, and the vegetarian caterers Earth's Bounty. The guests agreed the food was tasty.

The bride was radiant.

Ring in the New Year with babies, families and romance!

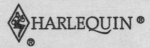

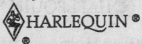

Heartbreak RANCH

Four generations of independent women...
Four heartwarming, romantic stories of the West...
Four incredible authors...

Fern Michaels
Jill Marie Landis
Dorsey Kelley
Chelley Kitzmiller

Saddle up with Heartbreak Ranch, an outstanding
Western collection that will take you on a whirlwind
trip through four generations and the exciting,
romantic adventures of four strong women who
have inherited the ranch from Bella Duprey,
famed Barbary Coast madam.

Available in March,
wherever Harlequin books are sold.

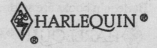

HARLEQUIN ®

HTBK

Harlequin and Silhouette celebrate
Black History Month with seven terrific titles,
featuring the all-new *Fever Rising*
by Maggie Ferguson
(Harlequin Intrigue #408) and
A Family Wedding by Angela Benson
(Silhouette Special Edition #1085)!

Also available are:
Looks Are Deceiving by Maggie Ferguson
Crime of Passion by Maggie Ferguson
Adam and Eva by Sandra Kitt
Unforgivable by Joyce McGill
Blood Sympathy by Reginald Hill

On sale in January at your favorite
Harlequin and Silhouette retail outlet.

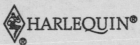